HOPE
AT THE
OCEAN'S EDGE

CHANTAL J. MACDONALD

SELAH PRESS PUBLISHING
NASHVILLE, TENNESSEE

For Jeremy,

Thank you for believing in this dream.

Prologue

Small, icy flakes whipped through the air creating a dazzling, white tapestry across the dark landscape. The beauty of the night was a stark contrast to the havoc the snow was wreaking on the highways. Small flakes, big storm. At least that was what nine-year-old Sadie Jones' parents always said. This proved to be no different as the whiteout conditions worsened making visibility poor. Her dad, Mike Jones, sat behind the wheel of the family's SUV navigating the treacherous roads. His wife, Cora, beside him checking the weather updates on her phone as they drove the two-hour distance from the city of Halifax back to their hometown of Lunenburg, Nova Scotia.

For Christmas, Sadie's parents had given her tickets to go see Rodgers and Hammerstein's *Cinderella* at the Neptune Theatre in Halifax the first weekend in February. Sadie was a bookworm who was drawn to happily-ever-after stories, with *Cinderella* being her long-time favourite. She had been beside herself with excitement at the thought of that being her first real-life musical and waited very impatiently for the date to arrive. So, when the winter weather threatened to ruin their special weekend away to the big city, her dad assured her that "a little snow wouldn't stop these Maritimers."

Mike was an average dad in every sense of the word. He was average height and had an average build. It wasn't that he was overweight, but the pouch that protruded ever so slightly above his belt revealed that his love for pizza all too often won out over his occasional bandwagon purchases of the latest exercise craze. His sandy blond hair was cut in a short, simple style. Bright blue eyes peered through black framed glasses that perched on his wide nose. His eyes almost always carried a glimmer of mirth. Mike Jones was not a man to let worry or concern cloud his heart or mind. He was open. Open to optimism, open to conversation, open to learn, open to people. In his opinion, people always had good intentions. But it was his warm smile and gentle demeanour that made him almost instantly loved by those who met him. His students at the local middle school where he taught science appreciated his quirky charm and slightly awkward humour. No doubt, he was one of the more beloved teachers at Elmwood Middle School.

Sadie adored him.

"It's saying up to 40cm overnight," Cora informed them, reading from her phone. She turned slightly over her left shoulder to toss Sadie a smile. "Looks like a snow day tomorrow." Sadie was the spitting image of her mother. Cora was a classic beauty. She was thin and petite and graceful. Her auburn curls were cut short, resting just above her shoulder in a stylish beach-washed bob. She had dark, chocolate brown eyes, the only significant difference from her daughter whose bright blue eyes mirrored her father. When she was little, Sadie's mother would often dress the two of them alike. Laughing, she would say that since Sadie had no siblings, it was her maternal right to incorporate matching ensembles into their lives however she chose. And she often chose outfits in bright pink.

Cora worked as head pharmacist at the drugstore downtown. Hard work and long hours in Sadie's early years meant that Cora now had more flexibility with her schedule. It allowed her to be more present on weekends and at family outings and school events. Sadie loved having parents who prioritized time together. She had classmates whose family lives looked quite different. Even at nine years old Sadie was aware of the privilege of having two parents who were still married and enjoyed each other's company.

Friday night pizza and game nights were Sadie's favourite. They were also a favourite of her best friend, Dawn. Dawn's dad left when she was five, leaving her mom to raise and support two young children. As a nurse, Dawn's mom worked shifts, which meant that she could end up working all hours of the day or night. As a result, Dawn and her brother, Dylan, spent much time visiting their friends. Sadie loved when Dawn was at her house. It was like having a built-in sister, even if that meant she also occasionally inherited an annoying little brother. As they drove, Sadie found herself reminiscing about one particular Friday game night that Dawn and Dylan were visiting. Sadie had been moments away from successfully completing a precarious Jenga move when Dylan jumped out from behind a wall wearing a gruesome Halloween mask and growled at them. Sadie had let out a piercing shriek and, in her alarm, had knocked over the entire tower. She did not like being scared, and she did not like losing at Jenga.

The wind whipped against the side of their car drawing Sadie's attention back to the present. She peered through the back passenger side window into the darkness. There was a forest of trees lining the road, but try as she might to see them, they were made invisible by the snow. It was hypnotic watching through the window as they drove. The snowy vortex blasting the front windshield looked as though they were aboard a ship straight out of the Star Wars movies and about to jump into hyperspace. But snow was nothing new. Storms were a common occurrence in Atlantic Canada—even more so in the towns along the ocean, like theirs. In Lunenburg winters were long and cold. Some years the snow accumulated so much that it covered the windows of their bungalow.

To Sadie and her friends, snow days were the highlight of the winter. Children became expert meteorologists in the winter months. They closely watched the weather channels and studied the skies for any signs of flurries. When all else failed, they would turn their pajamas inside out the night before a potential storm in the hopes that the superstition would grant them a day off. If the weather cooperated with the kids wishes and school was cancelled, Sadie's mom would creep into her room, give her a kiss, and tell her that she could stay in bed a while longer. On any other day, Sadie would give anything for a few extra minutes of sleep, but on snow days her excitement made it nearly impossible to stay in bed. Since her dad was a teacher too, it meant that they would have the whole day together. As a pharmacist, Cora provided an essential service, so she didn't have the luxury of snow days.

Mike would always be in the kitchen whipping them up a delicious snow day breakfast feast, complete with hashbrowns, scrambled eggs, toast smeared with homemade strawberry jam, and his favourite—

bacon. He loved to cook bacon. He and Sadie would stay in their PJs all morning watching movies or playing board games. The afternoon was spent playing in the snow. If the snow was wet and heavy, they would make snowmen or build forts. If it was icy, they would go sledding in their backyard. If the snow was light and fluffy, they would lie on their backs and catch snowflakes on their tongues. Mike always said that snow days were a gift. All the work that needed to be done was finished the night before and so there was nothing to do except enjoy the day and the people in it.

It was lovely to think about, but Sadie's snow day daydreams were abruptly cut short as her father shouted for them to hold on. According to police reports, what happened next took less than a minute, but for Sadie it felt like an eternity. It was as though she was standing on the outside watching life in slow motion.

She didn't see the eighteen-wheeler as it rounded the bend a little too quickly and lost control, but with every muscle in her body Sadie felt the impact. The truck collided with the front of their SUV, sending the family flying forward, and propelled their vehicle into the mountain of snow lining the road. Apparently, the car rolled at least three times before it landed hard on the roof, wheels in the air still spinning. The transport truck laid overturned in the center of the road blocking traffic from both directions.

Sadie hung from her seat, tethered to it by her seatbelt. Blood poured from the gash in her head where it had ricocheted off the passenger door window. Glass from the shattered windows was littered across the ground. The moonlight caused the glass to glitter in the darkness—a striking contrast to the wreckage strewn across the snow.

Silence.

Her ears gasped for sound, but all they heard was silence. Sadie tried to move to release her seatbelt, but sharp pains shot through her neck and arm. She forced open her eyes. It was too much. Through blurred vision, she searched for a glimpse of her parents. The wreckage was all around her, so close that it took her breath away. But there was no panic, no hysteria, no ability to connect the details of what was happening. She felt a heaviness settle over her and suddenly was very sleepy.

Sadie closed her eyes allowing the silence to overtake her.

And the snow fell.

Chapter One

NINE YEARS LATER

Don't be late. Don't be late. Don't be late.

Sadie Jones flew out the front door, letting the screen slam behind her. Rushing down the steps, she nearly tripped on the untied laces of her scuffed, tennis shoes. She regained her balance and opened the door of her beat-up red Cavalier. Sliding behind the wheel and quickly tossing her backpack in the back seat, Sadie turned the key.

Silence.

She inhaled quickly. *Not today, girl,* she pleaded with the car. *You've got this. Come on.* She tried again, and the car sputtered and grumbled and stopped. More silence. Continuing to hold her breath, Sadie tried again. The transmission reluctantly turned over, and the car came to life. Exhaling, Sadie eased the car out of the driveway and navigated through the narrow streets of Lunenburg to Harbourview High.

The morning sun beat down causing beads of perspiration to form on the back of her neck. Sadie cranked open the driver's side window to welcome in the refreshing breeze. The air caught hold of her wild, copper curls as if asking them to dance. The curls agreed and began to bob and sway and twirl, eager to take advantage of the invitation. With her free hand, Sadie tried in vain to restrain the dancers, but they were persistent. Giving up, she turned her attention back to the road. It was a quiet subdivision. and the morning commuters consisted mostly of a few minivans toting young learners and silver-topped seniors off to meet at the local Tim Horton's for their daily community coffee. She was able to zip along without much delay—one of the few perks to living in a small town.

Sadie tried not to watch the clock and instead drummed her fingers impatiently on the steering wheel. She thought back over the train wreck of a morning. Of all the days to sleep through her alarm. Sure, she was tired from her late-night cram session. The extra hours of work and study had filled her previous two weeks, but she had no idea the depth of her exhaustion until her head hit the pillow. She had awoken to find the clock on her bedside table reading 7:45 a.m. Only thirty minutes to get ready and make it to homeroom before the bell. Thankfully her morning routine was quite low maintenance, and she was able to toss on a pair of faded blue jeans and her favourite thrift store Toronto Blue Jays tee without much thought. Aunt Lynn forced a banana into her hand on the way out, which she had promptly stuffed into her bag. No doubt it would be needed later in the day.

Looming before her was the first exam of her final semester of high school. As a general rule, Sadie excelled at all things academic. Her early love of literature and a desire to be a model child for Lynn and Jack had been keys to her success in school. Unfortunately for Sadie, anxiety often became master when grades were at stake. These finals carried exceptional pressure. Doing well meant good final grades. Good grades meant being accepted into a good university, which was her ticket out of this suffocatingly small town—her ultimate goal. And today's exam was the most stressful.

History.

It wasn't that she disliked the subject. She could easily get lost in stories about the past, but the dates, names, and events got muddled in her mind. It was a struggle to keep it all straight. Her own history was a different story. Those details were seared into her brain. No matter how she tried to get past it, this town and these people wore her story. They paraded it before her like performers decked in bold costumes performing an interpretive dance. She saw it in how they spoke to her, in how they treated her as a fragile porcelain doll that needed to be handled with care, in the way their eyes took on a sad, sympathetic cast when they looked at her. Sadie often tried to remind herself that their hearts were in the right place, but, oh, how she longed for a fresh start. For someone to see her for more than her past.

Taking one more deep breath, she pulled into the student parking lot of the school. Sadie swung open her door, grabbed her battered grey backpack out of the back seat, and slid out of the car in one fluid motion. Quick strides took her across the dewy grass of the front lawn and up the concrete steps of Harbourview High. She flew through the two yawning doors and nearly collided with Vice Principal Preston.

"Slow down, Miss Jones," she scolded. "No need to cause an accident this early in the morning." Her tone was gruff, but her eyes conveyed a softer message. Sadie had seen similar looks often over the past nine years. The sympathy churned her stomach, but she had long since grown accustomed to it. "And tie your shoelaces," the vice-principal added.

Sadie immediately slowed her pace and nodded her head politely. "Yes, Ms. Preston. Have a good morning." She knelt to quickly tie her shoes and then proceeded to walk down the hallway as quickly as she dared, slipping into room 103 just as the homeroom bell rang out over the P.A. system.

As Sadie handed her exam papers to the teacher at the last possible moment allowed—three hours later, she was reminded of a line from one of her more recent reads, *The Color Purple*. "Time moves slowly but passes quickly." Time had certainly passed quickly as she struggled to regurgitate the last semester's worth of information into correct answers and coherent paragraphs, and yet the hours had dragged on to the point of monotony. Sadie massaged her right hand, which was cramping from holding the pen so tightly. It didn't matter anymore. She felt only relief as she gathered her belongings and moved to the hallway. There was nothing more that she could do except to begin preparations for the next one.

Sadie was on her way to drop her books in her locker and retrieve the necessary supplies to prepare for her next exam, advanced calculus, when she felt someone sidle up to her. "Was that as difficult for you as it was for me?" the voice spoke. Sadie turned and looked into the bright blue eyes of her classmate and best friend, Dawn Steeves.

Dawn was Sadie's nearest and dearest friend. They had been joined at the hip ever since Dawn had convinced Sadie to let her style her hair with safety scissors in preschool. Although Sadie's mother had been mortified at the resulting angular bob, Sadie hadn't been concerned. She'd made a friend. The haircut seemed like a suitable exchange for such a gift. For fourteen years, Dawn had been creating elaborate schemes, and Sadie had been tagging along for the adventures.

Dawn was effortlessly beautiful. Long, pin-straight, nutmeg hair framed her heart-shaped face. She was a style icon, at least in Sadie's eyes. Money was tight for the Steeves', so Dawn, like Sadie, was not attired in the most expensive luxury brands. The challenge of stretching her budget with unique thrift store finds was exciting to Dawn. Her style was a mix of vintage and bohemian. Curvier than Sadie, Dawn had confided more than once that her figure made her self-conscious. She preferred to err on the side of more modest clothing and often would style herself in flowy tops or skirts and lots of layers.

Dawn's personality, like her style, gave off an almost magical charm. Self-confidence derived from years of needing to fend for herself while her mother worked long hours paired with a bubbly, extroverted personality made her a force to be reckoned with. Dawn's greatest weakness was that she had a tendency to be a little boy crazy. Perhaps more than a little. It had gotten her into trouble more than once. Her mom didn't have the time, nor the energy, to monitor Dawn's dating life closely, and so dating rules, in Dawn's eyes, were simply suggestions. At just seventeen, Dawn had already burned through countless boyfriends. None were serious and no boy ever interfered with her friendship with Sadie. Dawn was fiercely loyal in that regard.

"Earth to Sadie," Dawn said waving a hand in front of her friend's face. "You still with me?"

Sadie shook her head and focused on her friend. "Sorry, my brain was still stuck in history. What did you ask?"

"I wanted to know if you found that exam as difficult as I did," Dawn repeated.

"Well…" Sadie began as she stopped and reached into her backpack, groping for the banana she had stashed there earlier. Hunger pains had made her stomach protest in loud and embarrassing gurgles.

Dawn cut her off. "Please say that it was hard, because I'd rather live in denial if not."

"It was challenging. Truthfully, I don't know how I did. I thought I knew most of the answers, but those essay questions are a killer. Mr. Mason really makes you think, which I guess is the point." Sadie responded honestly. She shrugged, peeling the banana, "I'm just grateful it's over."

"Me too. I cannot wait to be done with all of the stress of exams so I can focus on the more important things, you know, like prom and graduation." Dawn began a rapid-fire of questions that Sadie did not have the answers to. "Did you finally find a dress? Have you figured out if you are going to bring a date yet? I know it was kind of last minute, but I finally sucked it up and asked Josh Benson. I know he's a bit of a goober, but better him than go alone. Right?" She paused awkwardly, looking sideways at Sadie, "I mean, not that there's anything wrong with going alone."

Sadie walked along quietly allowing Dawn to ramble about dresses, pictures, grad parties, prom queen, and a slew of other classic graduation traditions. The truth was that Sadie didn't really care about much about any of it. Sure, she was excited to celebrate the end of this era, but her idea of celebration was planning for a future that promised new and exciting opportunities rather than dancing or taking pictures with her high school peers, most of whom she had spent very little time getting to know more than at a surface level. To Sadie, graduation meant freedom, next steps, and independence. The mere thought of it gave her the strength she needed to endure the grueling week.

Dawn had finally paused long enough for Sadie to interject. "I haven't figured out all the details yet. I need to do well on these exams and then I can think about graduation."

"But you are coming to prom, right? I can't imagine being there without you."

"Maybe," Sadie said non-committedly. "Maybe not." They were at the parking lot now and she was leaning against the hood of her car. "How about I promise to at least come and see you all dressed up." She grinned playfully, "I mean I wouldn't want to miss an opportunity to see you dolled up on the arm of a goober."

Dawn laughed and swatted Sadie's arm. "I guess I'll take that, but I would prefer to have you dress up with me. I haven't given up on that yet."

Sadie just smiled and brushed her off with a wave of her hand. "Good luck studying. See you tomorrow!" With that she climbed back into her car, feeling significantly lighter than earlier that day.

The next four days passed mostly in a blur. Sadie's life became a whirlwind of calculus, English, chemistry, and accounting. She had barely slept, she was living primarily off of Swedish berries and root beer, and she had worn the same jeans every day that week. Her brain was on overload when she finally handed in the last exam. The moment the paper left her hand it was as though imaginary weights were lifted from her body. She felt physically lighter, almost buoyant. This was it. There was no more to be done in her high school career. The feeling was exhilarating. Sadie was torn between wanting to faceplant in her bed and sleep for an entire day or celebrate with an extra-large gooey brownie sundae.

The bed won as Sadie returned home and collapsed into her pillows, barely registering that she was still wearing her sneakers. She awoke several hours later to Aunt Lynn gently rubbing her shoulder. "Supper is on the table, dear, if you are hungry," her aunt said. "I imagine that you could use a hearty meal given the way you've been eating this past week." Her tone wasn't accusatory, but rather sincere. Aunt Lynn was such a kind-hearted woman she wouldn't know how to be overly critical. She exited Sadie's room soundlessly, but left the door open as an invitation.

Since the death of her parents on that fateful day more than nine years ago, Sadie had lived in the care of her aunt and uncle, Lynn, and Jack Russell. They had been the obvious choice of guardians. Lynn was her mom's sister and closest friend. Lynn and Jack had been trying unsuccessfully for many years to have children of their own. They both had stable careers, Lynn a teacher and Jack a plumber. They were the only immediate family that lived in Lunenburg. Sadie's paternal grandparents and her dad's two brothers and their families lived in Ontario, not far from her dad's hometown of Sudbury. Her mom had no other siblings, and her mom's parents had both passed away when Sadie was a baby. Mike and Cora Jones' relationship with Lynn and Jack was always one of love and respect, and as such, Lynn and Jack were more than happy to honour Mike and Cora's wishes and accept guardianship of Sadie.

And yet, the transition still proved to be a difficult one. Death at any time is a cruel reality to accept. Sudden and tragic death can be even more crippling. Two days after the accident when Sadie left the hospital with only minor physical injuries and moved into Lynn and Jack's, grief moved into the Russell's home as a fourth and unwelcome houseguest. It cavalierly followed Sadie wherever she went—its grip on her heart often causing both physical pain and emotional outbursts. Lynn was completely heartbroken at her sister's passing, and she spent months navigating her own anger and depression. Jack mourned, too. He mourned for the loss of family, but also for the pain that it inflicted on his dear wife and niece.

Sadie's presence in their home was both a welcome distraction and a constant reminder of the loss. As a young girl, she struggled to find ways to handle her own grief while trying not to disrupt the preexisting equilibrium of Lynn and Jack's lives. She didn't want to be an imposition, and she didn't want to make things worse for Lynn. The couple assured her that she was loved and wanted and a blessing from God to them, but there were many uncomfortable and painful days as they learned to become a new family. It took years of grief counselling, both individually and as a new family, as well as much grace to begin to find peace and contentment in their new normal.

And then there was the town.

Small towns are notoriously cliché. Everyone knows everyone else, which means that, like it or not, everyone knows everyone else's business. Secrets are hard to keep, and the gossip train fueled by elderly people with little else to do often works faster than the internet. Word of the accident spread before police reports had even been released to the public. Jack and Lynn's phone worked overtime that night as they fielded dozens of calls from concerned family and friends.

But the suffocating closeness that results from small town life also brings many blessings. People in small town Atlantic Canada supported one another in the hard times and celebrated one another in the victories. Every weekend there was another hootenanny or benefit to raise money for someone struggling to pay medical bills or recover from a tragedy. There is a beauty that comes from truly living in community, but it also means that, at least temporarily, tragedy impacts everyone no matter how far removed they may be from those affected.

Lunenburg was no different. The community mourned with Sadie, Lynn, Jack, and the rest of their family. And like any typical East coast town, people responded in the only way they knew how—they cooked. Meals began arriving at the Russells' home almost immediately, visitors stopping by with condolences and casseroles. The town wept for Mike and Cora. They ached for Sadie.

Their sympathy, which was a welcome comfort in the beginning, eventually became unbearable for Sadie. Her private pain felt like a very public concern. Few people would be able to converse with her without pity in their eyes. She had come to loathe that look, the one that said, "How awful that your life is so broken." People would stumble over their words as they talked about family or holidays or storms or anything even remotely connected to that night. She knew that her peers at school didn't know how to act around her, and so they opted to keep their distance. It was always hard to know for sure what she had accomplished on her own merit and what was given to her out of pity. To the town, she would always be a victim. Sadie could not wait to be free of it all.

Regardless of the events of her past and how she felt about her hometown, Sadie was still stuck here for the time being. Groaning, she rolled over trying to coax her body to respond. The smells wafting up the stairs awakened her taste buds first. The spicy and savory scent of pot roast made Sadie's mouth water. No doubt there were sides of creamy mashed potatoes, gravy, and buttered corn—her favourites. Aunt Lynn knew. Her stomach pleaded with her for real sustenance with emphatic groans. Sadie planted her feet on the floor and stretched her neck, the muscles resisting. After days of being hunched over books and papers, it felt good to hold her head up and take in the surroundings.

Her room was small, but it was homey. A simple double bed was planted in the center of the room, adorned with a handmade quilt which had once belonged to her parents. To the left of her bed was a wide window which looked out over the front lawn. The long, plush reading seat her uncle had lovingly crafted at the base of the window was her favourite perch of the whole house. She had spent many hours on this seat. It was here that she was first introduced to characters like Anne Shirley in *Anne of Green Gables* and the Pevensies of C.S. Lewis' *Chronicles of Narnia*—some of her favourites. Those characters, and several others, had been her companions on darker days and her window into worlds of magic, mystery, romance, and far off places. In so many ways, books had been her safe place. One day, Sadie dreamed of walking the same streets as some of her favourite authors and seeing the world as they saw it. She had already visited the birthplace of the Anne stories—Prince Edward Island—considering that it was a neighbouring province. It was so lovely. Oxford, England, the home of Lewis, was a much loftier goal, but one she intended on accomplishing as she gained greater freedom in her life.

To the right of her bed was a tiny closet, filled with an assortment of loose-fitting peasant shirts—her go-to favourite look, a couple dresses for special occasions, and several pairs of denim jeans. A small desk and dresser sat next to the door, cluttered with hair products, note cards, jewelry, and other miscellaneous items. Sadie grabbed a floral scrunchie from the dresser, pulled her tousled curls into a loose bun at the top of her head, and let her nose guide her down the stairs and into the kitchen where her aunt and uncle were already seated at a full table waiting for her.

"Everything smells great!" she said, taking her seat opposite Lynn at a small round table. "I'm starving."

She paused before digging in while her uncle blessed the food, as was his custom. The meal tasted even better than it smelled. Sadie heaped her plate with all her favourites and then drowned it all in a creamy, brown gravy. Stuff that'll put meat on your bones, her aunt would say. It took a lot of restraint not to shovel the food into her mouth like a wild animal, but it was clear that this food was sustenance to her body and her soul. She felt the fog of the past week lifting.

Sadie smiled her gratitude as she chewed. Lynn seemed to appreciate both her appetite and presence at the table. Lynn and Jack were well-suited to each other. They were both modest, uncomplicated average Joes in a sweet and approachable sort of way. Jack had been a blue-collar man all his life; his cracked and calloused hands were a testament to his hard work. He was a tall man with a rotund belly that hung over this belt and thinning light brown hair that wisped behind his ears. In typical small-town fashion, Jack's approach to life and people was very open. He waved to everyone he met, his word was his bond, and he believed that one's upbringing was a strong indication of a person's character.

Lynn was equally accepting of people, but more reserved than her husband. She chose her words carefully and listened well. As a result, she and Sadie had weathered the preteen and teenage years well. When Sadie needed space, Lynn was quiet and did not impose. When Sadie needed a sounding board, Lynn would lend an ear. However, Lynn would rarely offer advice, instead affirming Sadie and her ability to make wise decisions. She was a slender woman, much like Sadie's own mother, but Lynn's appearance was less striking. A simple woman, Lynn's approach to her style was restricted to the essentials. She wore almost no makeup and her hair, which was almost always twisted up and pinned with a claw clip, was becoming more gray than brown. She did not believe in dyeing it.

Uncle Jack spoke first. "This is a celebratory meal. Congratulations on completing all of your requirements for high school. We—"

"We are very proud of you," Lynn interjected. "We have seen how hard you've worked for this. You know we love you dearly." She paused, looking at Sadie intently. "Your parents would have been so proud of you, too...." Her words caught in her throat as the emotion overwhelmed her. "How I wish they were here to see it for themselves." Sadie looked down and blinked away the tears that were beginning to form.

Jack cleared his throat. "As I was saying, we are very proud. Your grades and scholarships speak for themselves, but we wanted you to know that we think you are a remarkable young lady." He reached under the table, pulled out a wide flat, brightly wrapped box, and slid it across the table toward Sadie. "Now, it isn't the top of the line, but hopefully it will work okay. Congratulations, Sweetheart. You deserve it."

Sadie excitedly tore into the pink and yellow wrapping to reveal a new laptop computer—not the best money could buy—but much nicer than the clunky, dated one she had managed with for the last few years. Lynn and Jack must have dipped into savings to pay for it. "Wow! Thank you so much. This is perfect, and so generous." She hopped up out of her seat, gave her aunt a hug around the neck, and did the same with her uncle, planting a kiss on his rough cheek.

"Now we know that it's a little early for your graduation present, but we figured it will come in handy, you know, if you have any speeches to write." Lynn's coy hints brought up more anxiety in Sadie than excitement. The title of valedictorian had long been a dream she had been almost too afraid to verbalize for fear that she would be disappointed. Instead, whenever it was brought up, she would laugh it off as though it were trivial and not at all of any importance. The truth was that she wanted the recognition. She wanted the reward for her hard work. She wanted people to look at her with admiration and not pity. But, once again, she shielded her heart from vulnerability and laughed lightly at the suggestion.

"Oh, who knows what will happen, but I will definitely be able to put this to good use writing papers and doing research in the fall."

"Have you…" Lynn paused, looking at her hands as though they held her thoughts. "Have you decided on a school yet?" She was referring to the three acceptance letters which adorned the fridge. Sadie had applied to several post-secondary schools by recommendation of the guidance counsellor at Harbourview High. Ms. Batista told her that the added work may pay off in scholarships from various universities. The idea was to choose the one who offered her the most money. The problem that she now faced was which school to choose. Each of the three schools she had applied to offered her a substantial entrance scholarship, and each school promised to lead her into a different future. University of Toronto, McGill University, and Dalhousie University all boasted of excellent science programs, great choices for her dreams of working as a nurse practitioner, and all were big enough cities where she could more easily get lost in the crowd and start her life over again. If she chose Dal then she would remain in the same province and be close enough to home to visit any time she wanted. U of T and McGill in Montreal were bigger campuses in bigger cities, but the cost of travel would make it difficult to see her aunt and uncle any more than maybe once or twice a year. She was less concerned about visits home for herself and more for their sake. She was their world in so many ways.

Sadie had mentally pulled out her oft-visited pro/con list and was once again weighing the options when Uncle Jack placed a large hand on her arm. "Sadie, you doing okay?"

Sadie shook her head, allowing herself to snap back to reality. "Sorry. I spaced out. I guess I'm more tired than I realized." She stretched and yawned to prove her point. "I think I'd better turn in early tonight. I have a full day of work at the canteen tomorrow. Supper was delicious, Auntie Lynn. Thank you. And thanks to you both for the computer. I love it." She pushed back from the table, rinsed her dirty dishes in the sink, placed them in the dishwasher, and sprinted upstairs leaving her aunt's question about her university selection unanswered. A decision needed to be made about school, but it would have to wait until she had had more time to process all the important factors. This was her future she was talking about. It needed careful consideration.

As she returned to her room, Sadie paused on the stairs gingerly touching a framed photo of her parents that hung on the wall. They were at the shoreline standing with their arms around each other, the ocean in the background. This candid shot was captured as they attempted to pose for the camera. The ocean wind had grabbed hold of her mom's hair temporarily blocking her face from the camera. With his free hand, her dad was lovingly tucking Cora's hair behind her ear. A jovial smile danced across his lips. Sadie loved this picture. They were embracing the moment with one another, their smiles a reflection of their inner contentment. That kind of joy was what she wanted for her life. She wanted to finally feel okay with herself and her life when things weren't "picture perfect," and for that to happen, she needed to leave the place that was a constant reminder of her pain. She needed a new start.

Sadie touched her fingers to her lips, placing a kiss on each of her parents. "I love you," she whispered, and then mounted the stairs to bed.

Chapter Two

Saturday dawned dark and dismal. The clouds missed the memo that the dark days of exams and study were over. The dreary day beckoned Sadie to stay in bed, declaring that celebrations would wait for a brighter day. Unfortunately, her boss would not appreciate tardiness on their busiest day of the week. So Sadie reluctantly threw off the thick, handmade quilt and got ready for a full day of frying fish and waiting on customers.

Sadie cruised down Main Street toward the harbor. Quaint businesses lined the street. Although several of their exteriors were in desperate need of a fresh coat of paint, the dilapidated buildings were comforting. They were a snapshot into the past of this little fishing village.

Freddy's Take-Out, where Sadie worked, was no different. Its red barn-board siding had certainly seen better days, and the sign at the road beckoning visitors to come taste Freddy's award-winning battered fish looked like it hadn't been updated (or cleaned) for decades. The reality was that it probably was still the same sign. Her boss, Freddy Nelson, did not like change. He believed that customers frequented his establishment because they felt as though they could step back in time. For that matter, he had done very little in the way of updating anything during the past few decades. "I'm not messin' with something that works" he would always say. As a business model, it didn't really make sense, but one couldn't really argue with the man since the canteen was still thriving after almost thirty years.

Sadie liked working for Freddy. He was a fair boss, and a bit of a tease beneath a primarily gruff exterior. The canteen was a local hangout on Saturday afternoons, so it allowed her a chance to make money without feeling completely cut off from her peers. The one thing that she detested though was that she always left work smelling of grease and fish, which was not a necessarily pleasant perfume.

She arrived at the shop a few minutes before nine. Freddy's didn't open until 11 a.m., but the first couple hours of the morning were important for prepping the food they would need for the rest of the day. Surprisingly, Sadie didn't mind peeling 50-pound bags of potatoes and chopping cabbage for the coleslaw. It was mindless work, and she found that cathartic. Today it would serve as a good opportunity to process decisions about her future. Plus, she liked working with Sandy, a surprisingly hip fifty-something woman with a striking bob haircut and a straight-shooting personality. Sandy was Freddy's younger sister, and while she did not necessarily need the money because her husband was a commercial pilot, she worked each weekend because she liked to "keep her brother in line," she'd say with a wink. Working with Sandy made the time pass quickly for Sadie, and Sandy always offered Sadie helpful, though sometimes unsolicited, advice. Today Sadie looked forward to using her as a sounding board.

"Morning dearie," Sandy called from the front room. Sandy called everyone "dearie," even strangers. The screen door slammed hard behind Sadie making her cringe. *One of these days I am going to fix that,* she thought.

"Good morning, Sandy," Sadie returned as she grabbed her apron from the hook on the wall and slipped a hairnet over unruly, copper locks. "What's on the docket for this morning?" She eyed three 6-gallon buckets lining the back wall already filled to the brim with peeled potatoes. "It looks like you've already been busy." The comment was phrased more like a question than a statement.

"Oh, those. I think last night's crew did them up. It must have been a slower night." Sandy came around the corner and shrugged. "They will all need to be chopped though. And we are out of Freddy's sweet and sour sauce, so you'll need to make up a big batch and put it in the containers." She gestured to the counter where the supplies laid ready. Freddy believed in making everything from scratch. It was a bit more work, but the quality of his food had proved itself over and over again. "But that'll hold. First, sit and fill me in. How did exams go? Have they announced valedictorian yet?"

Sadie grabbed a wooden stool, pulled it up to the counter where she would be working, and sat down to face Sandy. "Exams were grueling, but I am happy with how I did. At least, I think I am. Results won't be posted until Monday. As for valedictorian," Sadie paused trying to figure out how to answer. She decided to be honest and confide in the woman who had been so helpful in the past. "They won't announce that until the marks are released. The truth is, I really want it. I want my hard work to be acknowledged, but I'm a little concerned that if I get it, I'm going to be a disappointment. I'm not the greatest public speaker, you know." She shrugged and continued. Now that she'd started, she might as well share everything. "And yet, I don't want to be given it out of pity. I want to earn it on my own merit. Given my past, how can I be sure that would be the case? Would I always wonder?" She was rambling now.

Sandy held her hand up in front of Sadie indicating for her to stop. "Now hush with that." She clicked her tongue disapprovingly. "There's not one person in that school, or this town for that matter, who doesn't know how darn hard you work at everything you do. You are one of the brightest young women I know, and if you are asked to be valedictorian you can rest easy in knowing that you've more than earned that title." She picked up a butcher knife and began to slice into an onion. "And as for a speech," Sandy continued, waving the knife in Sadie's direction, "well dearie, you just speak from your heart. Don't worry about saying what you think they want to hear. You just be yourself." She returned to her chopping and nodded for Sadie to grab a knife and join her.

"You're right, of course," Sadie responded as she grabbed a cabbage. Sandy's matter-of-fact, non-judgmental approach always brought a calm to Sadie's spirit. It was nice having someone she could talk to completely unfiltered. "Truthfully, I should be thinking less about being valedictorian and more about making a decision on where to go in the fall. I need to make my decision by next Saturday."

Sandy paused thoughtfully and looked out the window. "Do you see those birds, there?"

Sadie followed her gaze. "Yes."

"They don't worry about what to wear or what to eat. They just do what they were made to do, and God takes care of them." She turned to face Sadie. "There's no wrong decision. All the schools you applied to are great schools and all would provide you with what you need to pursue your chosen career. Just do what you were designed to do and trust God to carry you. But…" she paused again, leveled her gaze and spoke with authority. "Hear me clearly, dearie. You cannot run from your past. At least not for long. Eventually these things catch up to us. It's much better to face our mountains head on and conquer them."

Sadie was a little stunned and unsettled by how easily Sandy could see through her and cut to the deepest parts of her heart. She was right. Running from her past was exactly her motivation in all decisions about her future. But facing her past was simply too painful to relive, and even though she had grown up in the loving home that Lynn and Jack had provided, it didn't change that fact that she was an orphan. She had survived, and her parents didn't. She'd spent years mastering the art of burying her deep hurts and acting as though everything were fine while she kept people at a safe enough distance so that she wouldn't get hurt again.

Sandy was right about another thing, too. All three were great schools and would provide her with an excellent education. Maybe she was overthinking it all. "Thanks for the advice, Sandy. I'll let you know what I decide."

The two worked quickly, chopping cabbage, grating carrots, mixing sauce, and using a sharp fork to skewer potatoes and run them through an industrial grade fry chopper. Before long, it was time to open. Sadie ran the order window while Sandy managed the grill. They were a good team and managed efficiently for the next three hours as customers lined up for their weekly order of fish and chips, or lobster rolls and fries, or burgers and onion rings. By 2 p.m. when Freddy popped in, Sadie was ready for a break.

"Sadie, would you take these letters down to the post office?" Freddy said as he passed her a small stack of mail. "When you're done, you can take your break. I'll cover the window until you come back." He quickly shooed her toward the back door.

Sadie grabbed her lunch bag and her sweater and headed out the back, letting the door slam behind her. Thankfully the rain was holding off, but the clouds were still foreboding. They promised to quench the thirst of the eager foliage later in the evening. In spite of the gloom of the day, it was quite humid. Sadie paused to tie her sweater around her waist and then quickened her pace to the post office. It was only a short walk, but she wanted to maximize her lunch break. She loved to sit at the dock and people-watch as she ate.

She was skipping up the steps to the post office door when a car horn tooted down the street. Sadie turned her head to see what was happening and simultaneously crashed into what felt like a brick wall. The letters went flying as she fell backwards and landed hard on her posterior.

With a groan, Sadie rubbed her tender backside. *That's going to leave a mark*, she thought and then began to hastily retrieve the paper projectiles. The brick wall that she had crashed into was in fact a person, not actually a wall. The young man with whom she had collided leaned over and helped her rescue the last errant letter. "Man, I am so sorry about that!"

the voice apologized. "I was checking a text on my phone and totally not watching where I was going."

"Obviously," muttered Sadie. Looking up, she found herself staring into the eyes of a very attractive, and oddly familiar young man. His build was solid, which would explain the immovable force with which she'd just collided, and he was wearing light-washed jeans paired with a red and white baseball tee. His eyes were the darkest brown she had ever seen. Staring into them felt as though she were swimming in a pool of rich, dark chocolate—and she loved chocolate. At the moment, those pools held a look of sincere concern.

He met Sadie's eyes with a level gaze and seemed to be searching them for something. His look warmed her and yet made her feel vulnerable. It was as though he was peering into the recesses of her heart and rifling through the pages of her life story. She broke the gaze first, looking down at her feet. It had only been a moment, but it felt like time stood still. "Honestly," he paused, speaking more earnestly this time. "Honestly, I am very sorry. Are you hurt? Is there anything I can do for you?"

His concern softened Sadie's irritation, but also made her a little self-conscious so she opted to try and play it cool. "I'm fine, but I'm going to need your name and number for insurance purposes." Sadie internally grimaced. *Not cool. The complete opposite of cool.* That was not the witty comeback she'd been hoping would bounce off her tongue.

The young man stared at her for a moment and then let out a little chuckle, which grew into a full-on belly laugh. It was a hearty laugh that warmed her all the way to her toes. "Nice one." He extended his hand to her and introduced himself. "Glad to see you're okay. I'm Tom. Tom Carter."

Sadie met his handshake and smiled at him, "Sadie Jones."

Tom held onto her hand and looked her squarely in the eyes. There were those chocolate pools again. Sadie broke his gaze for the second time and scuffed her toe on the ground. It was difficult to keep a level head when he looked at her that intensely. "You look really familiar. Do I know you?" He questioned.

"I don't think so," she offered. "But you look familiar too. Do you go to Harbourview High?" Sadie doubted that was it since it was such a small school and she basically knew everyone, at least enough to recognize them on the street.

"No, I graduated last year from Halifax West High School. I wasn't sure what I wanted to do after school, so I decided to take a year off to work for my uncle fishing lobster. He owns a fishing boat." Tom gestured down the road toward the water. "It must be something else. Do you play ball?"

Now it was Sadie's turn to laugh. She didn't know what type of "ball" he was referring to, but it didn't matter. Sports were a big "nope" for her. Sadie had the coordination of a gazelle on ice. It just didn't work. Not only did she lack any notable athletic ability, but sports simply held very little interest for her. Sure, she had attended various games throughout the years, but only as a social event and only because Dawn would drag her to them. Dawn, on the other hand, took a keen interest in all things sports—provided there were boys playing. Thinking about her boy-crazy best friend made her smile. *If Dawn could see me now, she would lose it!* Sadie offered Tom the best answer she could think of. "I am really good at dodgeball. You know…because I'm great at running away from the ball." She laughed again at her own self-deprecating humour.

Tom smiled too. Then he snapped his fingers as a realization dawned on him like a lightbulb being turned on. "Freddy's," he asserted. "I've seen you working there."

Sadie nodded. "You're right. I work Saturdays." She remembered now seeing him come by a couple times with some other young guys. The talk of the canteen snapped her back to her responsibilities and quickly dwindling lunch break. "Speaking of, I need to drop these off at the post office," she fanned the recovered letters, "and get back to work."

Tom stepped to the side, spreading his arm as a gentlemanly gesture for her to pass. "It was nice *bumping* into you," he emphasized and chuckled at his own pun, adding, "You know, if you're free later you should come check out our ball game at Dodger's field. We play the Pacers at six."

Sadie was flattered at the offer but didn't want to read too much into it. She simply said, "Thanks! See ya," and walked past him into the post office but heard him call out behind her.

"Oh, and you might want to take off your hair net."

Sadie froze. Reaching up to her head she discovered he was right. She'd forgotten to remove it. Mortified, Sadie ripped it off her head and stuffed it into her pocket. Her whole body blushed bright pink from embarrassment. *Great*, she thought. *A boy actually notices me, and it's because I look like the lunch lady.* Still, he hadn't teased her about it or made her uncomfortable. In fact, she appreciated that he hadn't let her walk around town with it on. Sadie felt her blood pressure return to normal. Maybe the situation wasn't completely hopeless.

The rest of the workday passed quickly as a steady stream of customers kept her and Sandy busy. By the time that six o'clock rolled around, Sadie reeked of grease, sweat, and seafood—a repugnant combination. As she passed her apron off to the night shift staff and said good night to Sandy, Sadie felt an internal battle beginning to wage. Tom had said his game started at six which meant she could still catch most of it. The field was just around the corner. She was tired and felt gross. Going home was the easier option. She wouldn't mind a shower and a quiet evening with her most recent romance novel. But, the thought of seeing Tom again warmed her. If she were being honest, the intrigue of the potential was appealing. Sadie sat in her car chewing her thumbnail— what she always did when she was making decisions. Intrigue won out. Quickly texting Aunt Lynn to let her know that she'd be late, she turned her car in the direction of the ball field.

The parking lot was three-quarters full. As she eased her car into an available space, doubt began to settle on Sadie. She was looking and smelling less than fresh. She didn't know anyone else at the game. Shoot, she hardly knew Tom. She'd spent too many nights with her head buried in a romance novel for her to believe that this was anything more than a friendly invite. Sadie was about to cave to her indecisiveness and head home, but just as she slid the keys back in the ignition a rap on her window made her jump out of her seat. Her hand flew to her chest, and it took a moment before she could catch her breath and regain her composure. Sadie hated being surprised.

Smiling sympathetically on the other side of the glass was Tom. She opened the door and stepped out into the evening air.

"Sorry about that," Tom apologized. "I didn't mean to startle you. We really need to work on our meetings."

Sadie smiled and nodded. "I just scare easily, no harm done. Shouldn't you be on the field though?" she asked.

"Yeah, the game's started, but we needed an extra glove. I was grabbing a spare from my truck when I saw you pull in." he explained. "Glad you could make it. Come on, I'll walk you in."

Sadie, now feeling committed to staying, quickly reached into the back seat of her car and grabbed a navy pullover sweatshirt to guard her against the evening chill and to guard others against any lingering fishy odours. At the base of the spectator stand, Tom and Sadie parted ways. He jogged to the outfield with the rest of his team and tossed the spare glove to a tall, lanky blond guy. Sadie maneuvered her way through the other spectators to an opening on the bleachers. Tom took his position and then scanned the crowd looking for her, flashing her a crooked smile when their eyes connected. He looked good out there. It was partly his shaggy brown hair sticking out from beneath a battered baseball cap that he had turned backwards, partly his strong shoulders which filled out the red jersey, and a large part his confidence. It didn't take long to realize that he was an easy-going spirit and well-liked by the other young men on the team.

Sadie found herself quickly enthralled with the game. It was easy to root for Tom's team, the Raiders. Their obvious camaraderie and light-hearted banter with the opposing team was fun to watch, and the game ended up being a bit of a nail-biter. Sadie wasn't sure of the rules of the game and had to ask a gentleman sitting next to her exactly what was happening a couple times, but the two teams were neck and neck until the end. They went into extra innings and the Raiders claimed their victory with a home run hit.

As the team celebrated and the crowd began to disperse, indecision once again settled on Sadie. *Now what?* she thought. *Should I wait around to talk to him? Or is that too much?* She didn't want to be presumptuous and assume that this had been any more than a friendly invite. Opting to leave Tom to celebrate with his friends and not wanting to linger awkwardly, she headed to her car.

"Sadie, wait up," Tom said as he called after her. "You're not leaving, are you? The team and some other friends are heading out for pizza to celebrate. You're welcome to join us," he offered.

As appealing as more time with him sounded, Sadie knew that she wouldn't feel comfortable getting to know Tom in such a public setting. Not to mention that it had been a long day already and her aunt would be expecting her back soon. "Thanks, but I really should be getting home. It was a great game though. I don't come to many games, and I don't pretend to know all the rules, but that one had me on the edge of my seat. I appreciate you inviting me," she said.

"For sure," Tom smiled. "It was really nice officially meeting you today, Sadie Jones." He paused and looked at her again. Really looked at her. It was so unnerving when he did that. It made her feel vulnerable, and yet somehow safe. He took off his ball cap and ran his fingers through his hair. He put the cap on backwards and stated decisively, "I like you. There's something about you that is very intriguing. I'd like to spend more time with you."

Sadie was completely taken back. Tom wasn't following any of the "rules of romance" that she had read about. Leading men in her books or boys from her school tended to be aloof and disconnected with their feelings in the beginning. They played games to determine whether they were interested in a girl. She didn't know how to respond.

"You just met me. You don't even know me."

"Then let me get to know you."

"I…" Sadie began.

"Wait, don't say anything yet," Tom interrupted. He started to reach for her hand, decided against it and shoved his hands in his jean pockets. "You're right. We don't really know each other. I'm going to be hanging out with some people Thursday night at the bowling alley around 7 p.m. Why don't you come? If I'm a complete noob, then there's no pressure and you can just fake sick and bail." He smirked at her.

She considered the proposition. Thursday was prom night. She didn't have a date and hadn't planned on going anyway. If she met up with Tom, she would have time to see Dawn off, but would have an excuse not to be pulled along as a third wheel. "Alright, I'm in. But, if you are a complete noob, as you say, then I'd just say so and leave. I'm not one to fake anything, especially not to protect the ego of a noob." Sadie gave him a level stare and Tom laughed at her honesty.

"Deal," he said, extending his hand for a handshake.

Sadie placed her hand in his and tried hard not to think about how nice it felt. Thursday couldn't come soon enough.

Chapter Three

"I'm still bummed that you won't be with me tonight," pouted Dawn as she swept eye shadow across her eyelids. "It's our last big school dance."

"You know I was never really into them. Plus, I wasn't about to be a third wheel with you and Josh," Sadie explained.

Dawn waved her off and then gestured for her friend to zip up the back of her dress. "Sounds like you could have convinced Tom to come with you easily enough." She stepped back and admired herself in the full-length mirror and then turned for Sadie to take in the completed package. "There. How do I look?" she held out her arms like a modern-day Cinderella and gave a twirl.

Dawn was stunning. Her nutmeg hair cascaded over her shoulders in loose ringlets. It was partly pulled back into a braided crown on the top of her head. Light touches of makeup made her green eyes sparkle. A floor-length lavender dress adorned her hour-glass figure. It was sleeveless with a beautiful, sweetheart neckline and a slit that ran from her left foot to just above her knee. Dawn had accented the dress with a dainty teardrop necklace and silver bangle. Her best friend was radiant.

"You are beautiful, Dawn" Sadie responded sincerely. "Inside and out. You're going to knock Josh's socks off."

"Good," Dawn replied. "That's what I was going for. Now we have a few minutes before he gets here. Tell me again about Tom."

Sadie laughed. "I've already told you everything. Twice. I am keeping my expectations for tonight low. He could turn out to be a weirdo who wears socks and sandals."

Dawn rolled her eyes. "Firstly, you know that's in style right now. Secondly, who cares if he's a little weird as long as he's a nice guy and you give him a chance. To be honest, I'm proud of you. This is more interest than you've shown in anyone in a long time." She paused. "Are you going to tell him about being named valedictorian?"

Sadie had wondered the same thing. Most likely the topic wouldn't come up unless she brought it up, but she was proud of her accomplishment. She had received a personal phone call from the school's principal Mr. Murphy two days ago. That meant she now had only four more days to write her speech.

"I don't know. I don't want to sound egotistical," she answered honestly.

"You could never. Maybe if things go well tonight he will want to come to see you at graduation."

"Let's not get ahead of ourselves, Dawn. You know that meeting my aunt and uncle would be a big step—" Sadie paused and sat down on the edge of the bed, "for lots of reasons."

Dawn sat down next to her and took her hand. "I don't say this lightly, but in case this could actually go somewhere, he should know from the beginning. Don't let it build up into this big thing that you have to explain later."

Sadie nodded. "I know. But my parents have been gone nine years, and I still have such a difficult time telling the story."

Dawn pursed her lips and gave Sadie *that* look. The one that said someone felt awful but had no idea what to say. Normally that look would make her cringe, but this was her best friend. Where other people would fumble to find the right words and end up saying something to try and minimize her grief, Dawn would just sit in the moment with her and allow the feelings to exist whatever they were. It was a beautiful quality. Sadie was sure she would not have survived without her.

After a moment, Dawn squeezed her hand and hopped up. "Alright, enough about you. Back to me," she said jokingly. Dawn was always able to lighten the mood in any room.

Sadie laughed and stuffed any dark thoughts deep into the recesses of her heart. She cleared her throat and with a curtsy and her best British accent said, "Yes, your highness. Shall we descend the stairs and await your prince and his royal chariot?"

Dawn giggled and played along. "But, of course."

The doorbell rang, letting them know that "Prince Charming" had arrived. After dozens of pictures, the couple was off, waving to their adoring fans from the beater Chevy Cavalier chariot. Sadie then said goodbye to Dawn's mom and brother and headed to the bowling alley. She still had some time before she needed to arrive, so she swung by the library to return some books. A coy smile danced across her lips as she dropped the books into the return slot. There would be no need for fanciful literature tonight. Dawn was off playing the role of a princess, and now Sadie was about to take her own leap of faith in the romance department. Butterflies danced in Sadie's stomach. The real thing felt a whole lot riskier than that of her novels.

Sadie arrived at the bowling alley around 7:15 p.m. She had realized too late that she hadn't asked for many details about Tom's hang out, and she definitely didn't want to arrive before him. Their last conversation had been so startling that she had also forgotten to get any contact information from him. She and Dawn had tried to find him on social media, but he was a ghost. Nowhere to be found. That was certainly an unsettling realization and one that she intended to get to the bottom of.

The bowling alley was a hot spot in town, mostly because, aside from the movie theatre, it was the only place for good clean fun. The owners of the alley also owned a small pizzeria which allowed patrons to linger longer. They drew a sizable crowd most weekends, though unfortunately, a good many of her peers opted to spend their free time in parking lots, basements, or bridges creating their own versions of fun. At least, those were the rumours. That was not now, nor had it ever been appealing to Sadie. She didn't judge them; she just didn't want to be like them. Many of them were on roads leading nowhere, and her eyes were set on somewhere. She had dreams that reached far beyond this little hick town.

Sadie's eyes scanned the room. She spotted Tom in the middle of a group of people. *Not surprising,* she thought. *He's so friendly and likeable— of course everyone would want to be around him.* Confidently, she walked toward the group. Years of going against the grain had made Sadie comfortable in her own skin. She didn't mind the fact that no one knew her or that she had been invited as an afterthought.

Tom looked up and she caught his eye, giving him a little wave. A wide smile stretched across his face as he stepped out of the circle to meet her. "You came."

"So I did," she replied.

"I thought you might bail on me, and I realized I don't have your number. No way to hold you to it." He raised his eyebrows and smiled as though pleased with his subtle hint at a deeper connection.

Sadie didn't bite. Instead, she fished for other information. "You could have looked me up online and sent a message. I mean, if you were really concerned." She smiled innocently.

"Touché." He put his hands in his pockets and rocked on the balls of his feet. "I guess by now you've figured out that I don't exist in the virtual world. This is a weird way to start off a conversation, but the truth is that a few years ago I was a different guy than I am now." He suddenly looked very interested in the floor tiles.

"As in…" Sadie trailed off, waiting for him to fill in the blanks.

Tom exhaled slowly before responding. "I was a people pleaser. I wanted to be liked so much that I had a hard time saying no. Ended up that I fell into some pretty destructive habits. One of the worst was some online addictions. Pretty bad stuff, if you catch my drift. Then I found Jesus and everything changed. He pulled me out of the darkness that threatened to drown me. Eventually I became pretty convicted by what I was doing. I stopped it all, cold turkey, but I know that the temptations are real. Falling back into that world was a risk I just didn't want to take, so I shut down my connections to all social media."

Sadie was shocked. Shocked by his immediate transparency. Shocked by his honesty. Shocked by the mention of Jesus. Of course, she wasn't unfamiliar with the name or the religion. Her parents had been Christians, and she had been in a kid's program Sunday mornings when they were alive. Even now, she attended church each Sunday with her aunt and uncle, though she did that more out of respect to them than any personal conviction. Theirs was a small, traditional country church, and she was the only one her age that attended. Sadie usually spent those mornings in a hard pew sitting between her aunt and uncle, but miles away in a daydream. The truth was that she had closed herself off to the belief in a loving God years ago. Any supernatural being who would tragically take away both of her parents—parents who had professed to follow Him—was not one she wanted to be associated with. It was strange to hear Tom talk about Jesus so personally. "That seems excessive," she commented.

"It is pretty drastic. I spent a lot of time talking to Pastor Jay." Tom gestured to a man leaning against the wall talking to a couple of middle school boys. The man looked to be in his thirties. He wore a wide-brimmed cap, hoodie, and jeans. His style helped him to fit into the group, but the salt and pepper beard and laugh lines around his eyes were obvious markers of his maturity. "He is the youth pastor at the church where I ended up. Jay became like a mentor to me. We spent a lot of time talking about ways to protect myself from falling into those traps again. This was the best option we could think of."

"But you just said you'd changed." Against her better judgement, Sadie found herself intrigued by the story of transformation.

"And I have, but just because my desire to live better has changed doesn't mean that I won't be tempted by things or face challenges. The reality is that this world is messed up. If I'm going to navigate it well, I need to give myself the best chance." He shrugged. "It's not complicated, but it's not always easy either."

Sadie let his words digest. Tom certainly was not like any of the boys she knew at her school. He was straightforward, honest, and generally likeable. Her mind was telling her to turn and run. That getting mixed up with a Jesus-loving, athletic, fisherman was a bad idea. Her heart was drawn to him for some reason. She wanted to know more about who he was, both then and now.

Tom cleared his throat. "Okay, enough heavy stuff. Let's have some fun." He turned back toward the group of people he'd been talking with at the beginning, gesturing for her to follow. "I'll introduce you and then we can start bowling."

The group he referred to was a mix of guys and girls, all of whom looked shockingly young to be hanging out with someone out of high school. Sadie gave a friendly smile and did her best to remember names as Tom introduced the circle. "There is some more of the crew in the first couple lanes." Tom pointed to the left of the room. "And, as I mentioned, that's Pastor Jay there in the red hat."

Now Sadie was officially confused. Tom must have read her emotions because he offered more information. "I volunteer as a youth leader at Hope Valley Church. We usually meet there Thursdays, but this is our end of school party. Jay Porter is the youth pastor there."

"Ahh. I see." Sadie ran through a variety of emotions at lightning speed. First relief that Tom's best friends were not middle schoolers. Then admiration of him for giving his time to help out with these youth. Then anxiety over being a part of the night. She didn't belong there.

Being with Tom made it seem like she was there as a leader of the youth group, too. That, however, was not the case. She had nothing against volunteering. In fact, Sadie occasionally helped out at the local senior citizen's center as an activity planner, but this was different. A spiritual role model she was not. Her heart was closed to all of it.

Worrying about what they thought wasn't going to get her anywhere, she reasoned. She would just have to be as honest as possible and hope that no one cornered her or asked her any spiritual questions. *And talk to Tom. He should know this stuff makes me uncomfortable.* However, the truth was that she felt uncertain about spending any more time with Tom after tonight. Sure, she was intrigued by him. And she had thought about him every day since their chance encounter on Saturday. And she may have doodled Sadie Carter once or twice over the last few days. But this Jesus thing was a new development, and not one she was sure she could live with.

Tom gave her a quizzical look, as though trying to read deeper into her response, shrugged his shoulders then handed her a ball. "You're up next."

The match was tight, and the Sadie found the anxieties melted away as her competitive spirit took over. Tom's jovial banter from Saturday's ball game returned as he struck up a friendly competition with the adjacent lane. She was drawn to his energy. Perhaps his religion wouldn't be that big of an issue. *I'm going to church on Sundays anyway*, she thought.

It seemed Sadie wasn't the only one drawn to Tom. The young girls in the group were flirting with the older leader as innocently as only a middle school girl can. The young guys were watching Tom closely and doing their best to gain his approval. It was cute to watch, and Sadie wondered if she had ever been that way as a middle schooler. Tom handled it all with a humble ignorance. He seemed sincerely oblivious to his popularity.

Sadly, their team conceded defeat as the opposing team ended their tenth frame with two strikes. Rounds of high fives and pats on the back were shared along with some friendly trash talk and plans for a future rematch. Sadie, who was not typically competitive when it came to sports being acutely aware of her personal shortcomings in that area, was pleasantly surprised by how much fun she was having.

As the teams finished up their strings of bowling, the crowd moved to the round tables and chairs positioned in front of the pizzeria. Tom pulled out a chair for Sadie and gestured that she should sit next to him. Pastor Jay ordered pizzas for the group, and as they were being passed around, another competition ensued between some of the boys. They were challenging each other to see who could eat the most pizza. It never failed to impress Sadie how much a middle school boy could eat in one sitting. Though she enjoyed a good competition, she was happy to sit this one out.

Tom read her mind. "Where do they put it?" he said in a tone that sounded slightly impressed.

"Are you not joining in?" Sadie joked.

"Not this time. My metabolism isn't what it was when I was thirteen." He patted his perfectly toned tummy. "Plus, if I'm trying to impress you, I don't think stuffing my mouth with pizza would help my case," he said honestly, flashing her an all-too-cute grin.

Sadie blushed. Avoiding the comment, she gratefully took a slice of pizza from the box that had made its way around to their table. *Ugh. Mushrooms. Why do people ruin perfectly good pizza by adding mushrooms?* She subtly picked them off and flipped the conversation onto Tom. "So tell me about being a fisherman. Do you enjoy the work?"

For the next fifteen minutes, Sadie listened as Tom animatedly told her all about the world of lobster fishing. Apparently, it was grueling work. Early mornings, long hours, heavy traps, and understandably angry lobsters make for some difficult days, he explained. But it was easy to tell from his expression that, while he may not love the work, he did love being out on the water. Sadie could understand that. She had always found great joy living close to the ocean. "Fresh water was good for your body, but salt water was good for the soul," her uncle always said.

"You should come down to the docks sometime and I'll show you the boat," Tom offered.

She was about to agree in spite of her earlier reservations when Pastor Jay stood and asked for the attention of the group. "Okay folks. It's been a lot of fun this evening. Congrats on making it through another school year. Before we wrap up, I've asked Tom Carter to share a short testimony with you to close off the night. I know that you will give him your undivided attention as he comes."

Sadie was shocked. Tom looked at her and raised his eyebrows with a smirk as if to say he enjoyed surprising her. He stood and gave Pastor Jay a manly clap on the back as he passed. Taking a seat on a stool in front of the group of young people, Tom pulled a small book out of his back pocket.

Sadie shifted in her seat uncomfortably. What was he going to say? *Oh, I hope he doesn't mention me or why I'm here.* Her unease didn't last for long. As Tom began to speak, she found herself riveted by his words.

"Before I share a bit of my story, I want to read a passage from the beginning of the book of John. It's a part of the Bible, and it really helped me out of a dark time." He began reading.

"In the beginning was the Word, and the Word was with God and the Word was God. He was with God in the beginning. Through him all things were made; without Him nothing was made that was made. In him was life, and that life was the light of all mankind. The light shines in the darkness and the darkness has not overcome it" (John 1:1–5, NIV).

"I know it might sound a bit confusing, but that last line…that's one that I have come back to time and time again. I know a lot about living in darkness. You see, I wasn't raised in the church. I grew up believing that life was what you made it. When I started middle school, I was tempted by a life that promised to give me everything I thought I wanted—popularity, girls, friends. I wasn't in high school long before I caved to the temptations of that life. I started drinking and attending parties with the 'cool kids'." Tom made air quotes around the word cool. "That in itself is a recipe for potential disaster for a grade nine guy who hasn't developed good decision-making skills. But it got worse. I started partying every weekend, sometimes multiple times. I was lying to my parents about where I was. My grades started slipping, and by grade eleven, I was addicted to pornography." Tom paused letting the gravity of his words settle on the crowd.

Sadie was shocked—not just by Tom's confession but by the manner in which he was delivering his story. He spoke from a place of sincere remorse, but it didn't seem to carry a weight of shame. The rest of the group must have felt similarly because no one spoke or moved. They were hanging on to Tom's every word.

"I was a mess. I was spending my life trying to escape the reality of who I had become. I didn't want to drink; I needed to drink because I couldn't face myself. It was no longer about trying to be popular; it was a coping mechanism for the train-wreck my life had become. Then one day, a girl in my class, not even someone I knew very well, invited me to a concert at her church. I scoffed at her. I didn't do church. That was stuff for uptight losers, but that night as I was headed out to another party, I found myself driving toward the church. At first, I tried to tell myself that I just wanted to prove how lame they all were. The truth was that I was just so tired of the emptiness. I don't know how I found the courage to walk through those church doors, but looking back, I know it was God.

"The music was catchy enough to get me to stay, and between songs, the pastor spoke about how God sent Jesus in the middle of our mess to redeem us. That's just a fancy word to say that we owed and he paid.

"Here's the reality. Our world is messed up. Maybe you've given into temptation and are feeling trapped. Maybe things have happened to you that have hardened you and made you bitter. Or maybe you feel completely abandoned by God and you are left to deal with this broken world in whatever way you can. I was all of those things."

Tom readjusted his position on the stool and continued. "What I have learned is that God never abandons us. Quite the opposite actually. God says, 'I will never leave you or forsake you.' We feel abandoned because we walk away from Him. We were made to live our lives in relationship with Jesus, and when we are far from Him, life feels empty and lonely. Jesus fills the emptiness. He gives purpose. He gives deep peace in the middle of your mess. He doesn't promise that life will be easy, but He promises to love you unconditionally, in spite of what you've done or how far you've fallen. He promises to be with you."

Sadie shifted uncomfortably and looked around the room.

Tom continued. "The night of the concert I was stunned. God loved me. God had sacrificed His son for me. Why on earth would He do that? I was a mess. But for some reason, I was a mess, and he met me in the middle of it. My old lifestyle still held a lot of temptation and eventually I became pretty convicted by it. One night I just decided to quit it all cold turkey. It sure wasn't easy; there were a lot of difficult conversations. But through His strength, I turned my life around. He offers the same peace to you. If you want to experience the same kind of transformation, Jesus is offering it to you free of charge. All you have to do is open your heart to Him. If that is you, come find me after if you want to talk more."

With that Tom was done. There was no uber-spiritual prayer or elaborate conversion time. He simply passed it back over to the pastor and sat down as though he hadn't just dropped a bomb on the group. Sadie looked at him and raised an eyebrow. Tom smiled and shrugged. *How can you be so nonchalant about all this, Tom?* She thought.

Not long after Pastor Jay dismissed the group, Sadie made an excuse to leave.

"Are you sure?" Tom asked. "You don't have to rush away. We can stay and hang out." He looked so hopeful that Sadie almost changed her mind.

"I'm sure. I'm not really feeling that great. I think I should get home and get some rest." It wasn't a lie. Sadie's stomach had been churning uncomfortably since Tom had started speaking to the group. She needed space, time to think and process everything from tonight.

Tom conceded, "Okay, well let's at least exchange numbers so we can stay in touch." He pulled a thin, black phone out of his pocket. "I really liked spending time with you tonight, and I'd like to get to know you more." He looked at her intently. "You fascinate me, Sadie Jones."

Sadie's cheeks flushed. They exchanged numbers and she left and headed home, her heart heavy.

That night Sadie crawled into bed exhausted from the emotional rollercoaster Tom had taken her on. Her attraction to him was clearly growing. The quality of his character was reinforced by his interactions with those around him. He spoke to everyone with kindness and a straightforward sincerity. But the church side of him—that was something she hadn't expected and truthfully didn't know how to handle. And then there was his talk.

She buried herself in the covers of her bed and stared at the ceiling fan.

Her mind felt like the fan. Spinning in circles. Tom couldn't have known about her past because she had not found an opportunity to share it with him. Had he learned about it from someone else? No. It was unlikely that he had heard from a secondary source, or he would have brought it up. He was definitely a "walk in the front door" type of guy. So how could he have spoken so directly to her heart? Did he realize that his message had laid bare the deepest hurts she carried?

Abandoned. That was the word he used. And that was exactly how she often felt. Not that her parents had any choice, but they were gone, and she was here. She was the one left behind to deal with the mess, to figure out the world without them. God had abandoned her, too. He could have stopped the accident, but He didn't. How could Sadie surrender herself, as Tom said, to a being who didn't care enough about her to keep them safe?

Her heart was conflicted. In spite of herself, she longed for the peace that Tom spoke of. She wanted to feel as though she could finally accept what had happened as part of her story without needing to run from it. But it was just outside of her grasp. Silent tears streamed down her face as she fell into a restless sleep.

Chapter Four

Sadie breathed in deeply, jutting out her jaw so she could quickly exhale and blow an errant curl out of her line of sight. She was perched in the middle of a faded, brown, microsuede sectional in the living room. Nestled in the crevice where the cushions met was one of the coziest spots in the tiny room. On her knees she balanced her new laptop, whose screen held several open internet tabs all related to her three choice universities: University of Toronto, McGill, and Dalhousie. Sadie had put the emotional turmoil of last night behind her. She was in the final hours of needing to make a decision about which university to attend.

Uncle Jack was content stretched out across from her in his favorite reclining armchair. He had the television on the sports channel, but it was muted. He didn't like to miss an update. Auntie Lynn sat in a rocking chair next to a picture window that looked out into the backyard. Her Bible lay open in her lap, and she hummed a quiet tune as she rocked. They were both patiently being present with Sadie as they generously allowed her the space she needed to process. In their early days of counselling, they learned from their counsellor that being present would help navigate grief, and they had used this tool many times through the years. The counsellor had said that in grief, it is important to allow oneself the space to feel each emotion that comes. Healing is not a solitary moment, but a lifelong journey with many peaks and valleys. Allowing a loved one space to process without forcing them to be something they are not ready for is one of the best ways to support them.

In the quiet moment, Sadie looked up from the computer and took in her surroundings. Tiny dust particles danced across the air as evening sunbeams cascaded through the window. Hidden to the eye for most of the day, this was the moment for the almost microscopic specks to shine as they twirled and bobbed across the open space. It was mesmerizing. How could something as insignificant as dust hold such beauty?

In many ways, she felt like those dust particles—insignificant and at the mercy of whatever windstream wanted to move her. Sadie hoped that it would soon be her moment to shine.

Life had taken her on an unexpected and unwelcome wild ride. But in the same way that the sunbeams brought beauty and brilliance to those tiny flecks, her aunt and uncle had done the same for her. She was a bit of a mess, and her losses were still very raw, but she had a good home. Sadie was not oblivious to that fact. Jack and Lynn were good people and had been wonderful guardians. Together they had survived the darkest days, and together they had found new happiness as a family unit. Jack taught her how to bass fish. Lynn was by her side with gentle guidance as Sadie transitioned to womanhood. Every summer they would spend a week together at a cottage on the ocean. They had even taken a trip to Disney World together when Sadie was fourteen, complete with cheesy Mickey ears and family tee shirts. No, they weren't the parents she had been born with, but they had given her more love and support then many children ever receive.

Sadie breathed in slowly and allowed the gratitude she felt in this moment to soften the sharp edges of grief. Oddly, something Tom had said in this message came back to her, about how Jesus brought meaning to his life. She wondered for a moment if Jesus worked like the sunlight on the specks. Did He shine light on the people who were otherwise insignificant? Something deep in Sadie's heart yearned to believe that could be true, but there was still too much broken trust to accept that completely. She exhaled and once again watched the dust as it danced through the room. A peace finally settled on her heart about where to go to school.

"It's Dalhousie," she stated decisively.

Lynn closed her Bible and Jack turned off the TV. They got up and sat on the couch flanking Sadie. Lynn grabbed her hand, gave it three tight squeezes, and looked at her intensely. "Sweetie, are you sure?"

Jack jumped in. "We just want to make sure that you aren't staying close to home for our sake. We'd hate to hold you back."

"No," Sadie responded confidently. "I am making this decision for me. It's a great school with a great science program. I just decided that I wanted to be close enough to visit you both—lots. You are family, and I love you so much." Sadie paused, timidly smiling at Jack and then Lynn.

"It looks like we won't be converting your room into a home gym anytime soon," Jack joked.

Sadie chuckled at the thought knowing full well that Jack would never attempt any type of exercise regimen that didn't entail casting a fishing line. They laughed with her and squeezed her into a Sadie sandwich as she soaked in the peace of the moment. The decision was made, and with that came relief. Yet, deep down there was still a gnawing, unsettled feeling in her stomach, one that was completely unrelated to her school choice. As always, she pushed it away and enjoyed the embrace, squeezing them back.

"You know," Lynn said wistfully, "your mother would be thrilled at you attending the same university she did. I remember how proud she was to be a graduate of Dalhousie." Sadie nodded. The thought had crossed her mind, but she had tried not to let that be an influence on her decision.

"Let's go out for ice cream to celebrate," Jack declared. "Not that we need a reason to eat ice cream, but I think that this Dalhousie-bound valedictorian deserves a triple scoop." He chuckled. It was no secret to anyone that Jack had a sweet tooth, and ice cream was at the top of the list. The others quickly agreed, and they headed out to the ice cream shop downtown. Sadie was ready now to tackle a much simpler decision—triple chocolate fudge or cookie dough?

****

As Sunday morning dawned, Sadie was still thinking about her ice cream from the night before. In typical Jack fashion, he had convinced Sadie to get scoops of both flavours and an added topping of hot fudge. It was glorious. It made the fact that they all got caught in a sudden downpour worth it.

But there was no trace of rain clouds in the sky this morning. The sun greeted the new day with brilliance. It was the kind of sunshine that makes the treetops glow and the water sparkle. Sadie felt lighter this morning, no longer weighted down by indecision. Stepping into the new day, she inhaled deeply, allowing the fresh scents of spring to renew her hope for a fresh start. Sadie dreamed of riding the sunbeams across the clouds. Instead, she did a little two-step along to the morning bird's high-pitched melody as she, Jack, and Lynn loaded into the family Honda Civic and set off to Sunday morning service at the small Presbyterian church two streets over.

Making their way into the building, they stood in line behind two other families also arriving and chatting with the pastor. As was his custom, Pastor Ted greeted the church goers at the door as they entered with a hearty handshake.

"Mornin' Jack," he said with a wide smile, extending his hand to each of them. "Lynn. Sadie. So glad you could join us." Pastor Ted Wilson was a sincere and friendly man. It was hard not to like him. His balding halo of white hair was always neatly trimmed, and he wore thin wire glasses that framed his friendly eyes. Each week he sported a three-piece, double-breasted suit, the jacket unable to close over his hefty middle. He had been the pastor there for as long as Sadie could remember. He and his wife, Jill, were well-loved by the congregation and lived next door to the church in a tiny cottage home.

"Good morning, Pastor," Jack responded. "Beautiful day, isn't it?"

"It certainly is. Though it's always a beautiful day when we get to join together in the house of the Lord." They all nodded in agreement and headed inside to their usual pew, third row from the back, left-hand side.

The church was a humble, white building with broad front doors and adorned with a classic steeple. Hard wooden pews lined either side of the main room, often speckled in coloured light from the intricate stained-glass window on each wall. A tiny platform at the front housed a pulpit, an upright piano, and a bookshelf of assorted hymnals and offering plates. It wasn't an unwelcoming place, but time stood still here. Progress seemed only evident in the guitar amp that one of the members brought each week to use for the Sunday music. While it may have been outdated, Sadie attended without complaint because it meant so much to Jack and Lynn.

There was not much that they asked of Sadie, but this was one activity they had requested of her since she had come to live with them. They had done so much for her; it was the least she could do. She typically spent the hour and a half daydreaming. It was the easiest way to keep herself awake and looking semi-engaged. Sadie found the services to be long and dull, and so, instead, she allowed herself to become the daring heroine of her fantasies. Sometimes a handsome stranger would win her heart and ride off with her into the sunset. Sometimes she became a sought-after celebrity who would jet set to exotic destinations. Once she was even a professional chocolate taste-tester at an upscale chocolate factory in France, but that one ended up with her stomach rumbling loud enough for everyone to hear. From that point on, she avoided any food related daydreams.

No matter what was happening in her daydreams, she would stand and sing when asked or bow her head for the prayers. The service was only a ritual to her, as she had closed herself off to faith long ago. It was simply easier this way. There were a few peers at her school who boldly and angrily protested faith. They wore their atheistic worldview like a badge of honour, but the toxicity of their hate was off-putting to Sadie. She didn't want to be like them. She believed that she was a good person and that there was value in morality. She couldn't, however, justify a religion that spewed proverbs and sweet thoughts like you would see on a cross-stitched pillow. Life was too messy, too convoluted, for that kind of world.

As the service began and Pastor Ted made his way to the front, Sadie felt unsettled. Something was different today. The lightness she had felt upon leaving for church had been replaced with an unease that she couldn't shake. Nothing seemed any different with the church. Nothing was ever different. She shifted nervously and mused over what could be the root of this sudden anxiousness she felt. Was she having jitters over leaving home? No, she was thrilled about the new adventure. Grief again? No, today was a good day in that regard. Nerves over her valedictory address? Possibly. She still wasn't happy with anything she had written for her speech. *Can the speech really be affecting me like this? What else could there be?* She dried her sweaty palms on her jeans, took a long, slow deep breath, and counted backwards from one hundred by sevens. It was another coping mechanism that she had learned from her counsellor years ago.

Pastor Ted's booming voice interrupted her thoughts. "Welcome church. So nice to see so many of you out this morning."

Sadie glanced around. She mentally counted sixteen people, including their three. It wasn't a lot, but it was at least one more family than they usually had. There had been more than double that many teens at the bowling alley for Tom's youth group send off. Sadie inhaled sharply. Deep in her heart something clicked.

Tom.

Tom's talk that night was still rattling around inside her. The things he had said about feeling abandoned by God and trapped in your circumstances had hit home. Normally she was better at silencing the voices in her head that demanded attention. Emotions were things to be controlled, not things that controlled you. But she knew that, if she were honest with herself, her story wasn't that different from Tom's. Sadie may not be chasing popularity, but she felt empty inside. Tired. Tired of feeling guilty for surviving. Tired of feeling abandoned by her parents and then feeling guilty for thinking they had any say in the matter. Her heart ached with a longing that she could not seem to fill with a romance novel or dream of adventure. At least not for long. For the past nine years she had been emotionally running from the pains of her past and soon she would be running for real—away from this town and anyone who knew her story.

Sadie rubbed her chest over her heart. Thinking of her parents sometimes caused her heart to physically ache.

But Tom's solution to the emptiness was no help. God might be willing to meet her in the middle of the mess, but did she even want Him to? What kind of God would allow such tragedy to happen? No. If that's who He is, she did not want any part of it.

She opted to listen to Pastor Ted's sermon today. Her own thoughts clearly could not be trusted. He instructed the congregation to turn to the book of James and began reading in Chapter One. Sadie pulled out one of the Bibles from under her seat and opened it to follow along. She only found the passage in time to catch the last verse.

"Every good and perfect gift is from above, coming down from the father of heavenly lights, who does not change like shifting shadows" (James 1:17, NIV).

Pastor Ted looked out at the congregation. "Our God is a good God. Think about your life. We know that there is not a person in here who hasn't experienced difficulties. There is not a person in here who hasn't experienced some kind of pain or loss. But there is also not a person in here who hasn't experienced God's blessings in their lives. You have clothes to wear, a place to lay your head, a roof over your head, and food in your belly. The Bible makes it clear that every good thing that we experience in our lives is a gift from God."

Sadie thought about her own blessings. True, her life had not been easy. She had dealt with more than her fair share of pain and heartbreak. But she would be lying to herself if she did not acknowledge the ways that she was blessed. In their nine years together, she had two of the most loving and involved parents that a girl could ask for. The older she got, the more that she realized that this was not necessarily the same story for several of her peers. She had heard many stories of broken families, abuse, and strained relationships. Even after the death of her parents, she was blessed to be in the care of Lynn and Jack. She glanced over at them, both of whom were listening intently to Pastor Ted's words. They would never be able to fill the void left by her parents, and the three of them had faced their fair share of tension, but they had provided Sadie with a loving and healthy home. They were her family and she loved them dearly.

Sadie tuned back into what the pastor was saying. "But God has blessed us far beyond what you can see with your eyes. Yes, he can provide for our basic needs, like the Israelites wandering through the desert God can give you your daily bread. But his goodness extends far beyond that which your earthly body requires. God is not just good, but he is perfect. We will always fall short of that perfection. We are broken and messed up people."

That is definitely something that I can agree with, Sadie thought.

Pastor Ted continued, "And in his goodness God gave us the greatest blessing of all. He gave us his only Son. He allowed his Son, whom He loved, to be sacrificed for you. For me. So that we could, in all our imperfection and sin, be with Him in paradise."

Once again, Sadie found herself lost in thought. She spent the remainder of the service trying to reason her own past against the pastor's declaration. She had been in church enough to know the Bible stories and rules to faith on which the church is founded. When she was just six years old, Sadie had quizzed her mother about God and sin and the cross. One snowy night snuggled tight under the covers, her mother had shared in whispered tones the story of God's love. At the time, Sadie was in awe of it all and immediately asked to know how to follow Jesus. The moment was simple and sacred. Sadie had felt as though she were a part of a secret club, and that life would be easy in the protection of such a big God.

That moment was such a long time ago, back when her biggest problems were early bedtimes and skinned knees. The harsh realities of the world had hardened Sadie. Life was made no easier as a follower of God. *It just does not make sense,* she reasoned to herself. *If God is good and all-powerful, why couldn't He just take away the mess? Why did He need to sacrifice His Son for the world to be with Him? Could He not, in all His power, just make people better?*

Her mind was racing, each thought taking flight in a different direction. Each question only led to more questions, and Sadie was not interested in searching for answers right now. She was about to start a new chapter of her life, and she refused to be held back by anything from her past. So, she locked her unease and uncertainties away deep in her heart and refocused her mind on a task list for moving to Dalhousie. Sadie could always distract herself by planning for what needed to be done, and never was there more need for distraction than now.

Chapter Five

Church ended at the usual time and the Russells said their goodbyes and headed home. After a light lunch of sandwiches and watermelon, Jack and Lynn laid down for an afternoon nap. They were adamant that Sunday was meant to be a day of rest and were intentional about enjoying a slower pace. Sadie grabbed a notebook and pen and headed for her room. She still had not managed to write anything for her valedictory speech, and time was quickly running out. The ceremony was in two days. What she did have was a trash can overflowing with crumpled papers covered in rejected ideas. Nothing she wrote seemed sincere. Everything emerged as cliché or generic. She stared at a blank page once more willing the ideas to come.

Nothing.

"Ugh," she growled, flopping backwards on her unmade bed. "Why is this so difficult?"

From her desk, her cell phone chimed with a familiar sound signaling a text from Dawn. Sadie hopped up and opened the welcome distraction.

"Girl...Update?"

Sadie had gotten so caught up in the relief of her school decisions that it had completely slipped her mind to fill Dawn in on her post-grad life news. She quickly typed a message, her thumb hovering briefly over the send button as she smiled. Dawn was going to freak.

"Start looking at apartments, roomie."

Sadie followed the text with black and gold heart emojis—Dalhousie's school colours. Immediately a Facetime request came through on Sadie's phone. She pressed the answer button to reveal Dawn's beaming face. "Eek!" Dawn squealed. Her nutmeg hair was pulled into a high bun and her head was haloed by a sunshine-y bandana that revealed her round fresh face and bright eyes. Her best friend could always look effortlessly adorable. "Does this mean what I think it means?"

Sadie grinned back. "It does. I accepted the offer from Dalhousie. Looks like we'll be staying in the same city together after all." Dawn had earlier been accepted into the English program at Mount Saint Vincent University, a school only ten short minutes from Dal. She had already hatched an elaborate plan that involved a cute, two-bedroom apartment they would share smack between both schools, should Sadie decide to stay closer to home. Her plan also included coordinating bedspreads and weekly chick flick movie nights. But, to her credit, Dawn had not been pushy with Sadie about choosing Dal over the other two schools. Her bestie was slightly impatient, but very compassionate.

"That is *so* fantastic!" Dawn squealed again, her face much too close to the camera as her excitement grew. "I want to hear every single detail about how you made up your mind and start planning our apartment decor, but I need to run to get groceries with my mom. Chat more tomorrow?"

"Absolutely." Sadie gave a quick wave and was about to hang up when Dawn stopped her.

"Wait! Did you finish your speech yet?"

Sadie pouted and held up her blank page. "Nope. Still stuck."

"You need to stop overthinking this," her friend responded. "Just keep it simple and speak from your heart."

"That's exactly what Sandy said."

"Well, she's a smart woman then," Dawn winked and gave a little wave. "Good luck!"

"Thanks. See ya!"

Sadie hung up the call, grateful that she didn't need to unpack all the emotions that had led to her final decision. The day had proven to be emotional enough as it was. Grabbing her notebook, she hopped off the bed, cozied into her window nook and looked outside.

Maybe Dawn was right, and she *was* overthinking this. The afternoon sun felt lazy as nature slowed down and basked in its warm glow. A frisky squirrel bounded across the front lawn, froze for a moment, and then scurried up a tall maple tree. Suddenly Sadie felt the need to be on the other side of the window soaking up the warmth and beauty for herself.

Throwing a canvas tote bag over her shoulder stuffed with her notepad, pen, and water bottle, Sadie crept soundlessly down the stairs to the kitchen. She left a note on the fridge telling her aunt and uncle where she was headed, grabbed her sunglasses and keys from the top of the refrigerator, and headed out the door to her car. The docks were not that far away. Sadie always did her best thinking by the water. The water calmed her spirit. Every time that she sat near the shore, she would inhale deeply, the saltwater filling her nostrils, and it was as though until that moment she had been holding her breath. The nearness of the water melted away all the worries and noises and frustrations of her world so she could just…be.

Sadie drove slowly, as was the custom in this small town on Sundays. Edging her car down the narrow Bluenose Drive, she pulled into an open parking spot in front of a bright red building. Lunenburg Harbour featured several brightly coloured, aged buildings, which now housed businesses catering to tourists. It was still early in the season, so foot traffic was light, but by August the weekends would see hundreds of visitors, some in search of a taste of salty cod, some to check out the home of the Bluenose, and some to hear a lively sea shanty in the local pub. The Old Town Lunenburg was certainly distinct and its appeal, understandable. However, the charm of the small, fishing town had long worn off for Sadie. She was ready to widen her worldview, even if that meant simply moving to a bigger city nearby.

Locking her car, Sadie sauntered between the buildings to the end of the dock. She preferred to sit at the very end of the dock rather than on the benches along the far side of the water, that way it felt as though the water was all around her. Crossing her legs, she pulled her notebook out of her bag. She thumbed through the pages until she found what she was looking for. *Aha!* She thought, smoothing the page with the palm of her hand. *There it is.* A couple of years ago as she was reading *Anne of the Island,* Sadie was struck by the lines, as she often was with the incomparable protagonist, Anne Shirley. Sadie had recorded the words to look back on. She read them aloud:

…the Lake of Shining Waters was blue—blue—blue; not the changeful blue of spring, nor the pale azure of summer, but a clear, steadfast, serene blue, as if the water were past all modes and tenses of emotion and had settled down to a tranquility unbroken by fickle dreams.

Tranquil.

It wasn't a brilliant blue lake, but that was always exactly how the ocean made her feel. Hopefully today it would also help her to feel inspired. She really did not want to walk onto that graduation stage with a blank notebook.

"Sadie?" A voice from behind her caused her to jump. She did not like to be startled. Turning, she found herself looking at one very dirty pair of muck boots that just happened to be attached to one very handsome fisherman. Tom stood over her, his eyes smiling though his face wore a quizzical look. Outfitted in a red, plaid, button-down work shirt and tan-coloured oil pants, it was clear that Tom had either just left the fishing boat or was heading there now. They hadn't spoken since she left the bowling alley on Thursday night, save for a couple of funny graduation memes that he had texted her.

"Hey Tom! Fancy meeting you here," Sadie winced at her attempt at nonchalance. He laughed and extended his hand to help her up. She took her time, hoping to regain her composure at the sight of him. Once again, she found herself warming at his touch.

"I guess I could say the same. Who were you talking to?" He asked.

Sadie smoothed her shirt, and wrapped her arms around her notebook, holding it close to her chest. She hadn't realized that anyone was listening, and her cheeks flushed at the thought of having an audience to her monologue.

"Myself, I guess." Despite her embarrassment, she had to appreciate the humour of the situation. "Our chance meetings seem to always find me in the most unflattering positions." The breeze off the ocean blew through her curls causing the tousled locks to temporarily blind her. She tried somewhat futilely to tuck her hair behind her ear.

"Oh, I don't know," Tom shrugged as he walked past her and sat at the end of the dock with his legs hanging over the edge. "I find you charming." He looked up with a crooked grin and motioned for her to sit next to him. Butterflies took flight in Sadie's stomach. *How does he have that effect on me?* She wondered. Other boys had piqued her interest in the past, but none of them had ever cut to her heart so quickly as Tom had the past couple weeks. She hesitated for a moment before sitting down, leaving a safe gap between them, and waited for him to speak first.

But he didn't say anything right away. He just stared out at the water, taking it all in. Sadie watched him for a moment and then followed his gaze to the murky ocean waters by which she had earlier been entranced. For several minutes, they breathed slowly allowing the silence to resonate between them. It felt good to release expectation and awkwardness. She felt her muscles relax as she settled into the moment. Finally, Tom spoke.

"Oh God, you are my God; I earnestly search for you. My soul thirsts for you; my whole body longs for you in this parched and weary land where there is no water" (Psalm 63:1, NIV).

Now it was Sadie's turn to be confused. Was he praying? It seemed like a strange time to bust out into communing with God. *Why is he bringing up religion again?* she wondered. Not knowing how to respond, she stayed quiet and awkwardly waited to see what he would say next. Tom turned and shrugged again.

"That's one of my favourite verses. Psalm 63. I figured since you were talking to the water, I would too. Now we are even." He winked at her.

Sadie laughed. He was so good at easing the awkwardness and lifting her spirits. *Don't get in your head. He's a good guy. Give him a chance.* She decided to press in a little further. "Why is it one of your favourites?"

Tom paused thoughtfully. "I guess because I can understand where the writer of that passage is coming from. For years, I felt like the world was just exhausting. I was constantly searching for something to, like, quench my thirst. I tried all kinds of things, you know, but nothing really satisfied. I didn't realize that what I needed, what I was really searching for, was Jesus." He paused again, seeming to choose his words carefully.

"You know I've always felt drawn to the water." He gestured out toward the ocean. "What was the word that you used? Tranquility?" Sadie nodded and Tom continued. "Yeah, there's a tranquility to the water. But there's power in the water, too. I mean, you live here. You know all about that monument over there." He gestured toward the stone pillars behind them that held the names of all the Lunenburg fishermen who had lost their lives to their craft. Of course, Sadie knew it well. It was sobering to think about. "Lately when I'm out on the water it makes me wonder about God."

"How so?" Sadie asked.

"Well, God is a lot like the water. A source of immense power while also a still and peaceful refuge. It's crazy to think about all that He is capable of. A couple years ago it all clicked for me, you know. I was longing for something in my life in the same way that my body longs for water and my soul longs to be near water. When I found Jesus, He gave me the strength to quit my addictions and when I was still in His presence, I found a hiding place from the craziness of my life."

Sadie had been listening to Tom intently. Something in her soul echoed his sentiments. She was thirsty. She was searching. *Could Jesus really be the answer?* It seemed far too simple to be true.

"But what about the mess?" Sadie pushed. She wanted answers and Tom seemed to be a wealth of them. "How could you trust a God who would make you walk in a, what was it you said, 'dry and thirsty land with no water'?"

Tom corrected her, "parched and weary." Again, he took his time responding to her question. "I can't speak for everyone, but I guess I believe that it is because God never intended for it to be this way. Our world is so messed up. That's on us. God stepped into the middle of the mess and offered us a way through it. Being a follower of Jesus doesn't mean that you won't face hard days. In fact, just the opposite. It's pretty much a guarantee, but Jesus promises that you don't have to face any of it alone. He never wants us to feel alone or abandoned."

Sadie allowed his explanation to settle on her heart. She wanted to believe that it could be true, that God really did care about her pain. But how could Tom possibly understand? Her life had been ripped apart as a child. No nine-year-old should have to deal with the grief that she had. It simply wasn't fair.

Even though she felt an inability to truly comprehend Tom's faith, she wanted to be respectful of his story and his conversion experience. He had not been arrogant about what he believed, and she found it refreshing. "I think I understand what you are saying, and I think that is wonderful for you. I'm just not sure that I can believe it all for myself," she confessed. Sadie was a little hesitant about how much to tell him, but added, "Life has thrown me more than my fair share of blows."

Tom took off his ball cap and ran his fingers through his wavy hair before replacing it on his head. Wisps of curls stuck out from under the sides creating wings. Sadie thought it was endearing.

"I have a confession," he said nervously, rubbing the back of his neck.

Sadie adjusted her position so that she was facing him, one leg curled under her, the other dangling over the edge of the dock. "I'm listening," she said tentatively.

"I, uh, well, I may have asked around about you. Just with some of my family." Tom rubbed his hands together and seemed to be struggling to find the right words. "They told me about the accident. About your parents." Reaching across the space between them Tom gently took her hand in his.

"I'm so sorry that I found out this way and didn't give you the opportunity to tell me in your own time. But I want to be honest with you. I always want to be honest with you. And," he added, "I am so sorry for what you have had to go through."

Sadie was a little stunned. It shouldn't surprise her that Tom had found out about her past. This was exactly the reason she wanted to leave Lunenburg. The first thing that anyone associated with Sadie was that she was an orphan. Damaged goods. As the shock of his confession wore off, Sadie felt all the familiar walls go up, this time guarding her heart against Tom. There was nothing she could do about it, but now Tom saw her for who she really was. His sympathy was kind, but unwelcome. She pulled her hand away.

"Thank you for saying that. It's very kind. My aunt and uncle have been so good to me. I am very grateful for the life I have been able to lead." Her words were stiff and well-rehearsed. Tom must have noticed the shift in their conversation.

"I've ruined the moment, haven't I?" he asked. "Leave it to me to completely bumble things up with a cute girl." He took his hat off, readjusted it and put it on again. It seemed to be his nervous twitch.

Against her better judgement, a smile slowly stretched across Sadie's face. "Cute girl, huh? Moment?" She just could not help herself; he was so likeable and sincere. "Getting a little sure of yourself, aren't you, Mr. Carter?" she said with a tease in her voice. Tucking away any frustrations she felt over her circumstances, Sadie opted to extend Tom grace. It wasn't his fault that she was orphaned or the constant topic of gossip in this town. He liked her. He had told her that. She liked him, too. At least she was finding it very hard to stop thinking about him and his wavy hair and chocolate brown eyes. Sadie picked at a knot in the wood of the dock.

They settled into a silence again, each deep in thought. Once again, Tom spoke first.

"So, if you aren't here to take me up on my offer for a boat tour, what brings you to the docks?" he questioned.

Deciding it was a safe place, Sadie responded honestly. "I came here searching for answers." She shrugged. "Graduation is in two days, and I was chosen as valedictorian."

"That's amazing!" Tom interjected. "Congratulations."

Sadie held up a blank page in the notebook. "Unfortunately, this valedictory speech is the little engine that couldn't. I just cannot figure out what to say that doesn't make it sound like I googled 'how to write a valedictory address'—which I did, by the way."

Instead of offering advice on what to write, Tom questioned her. "What do you want to say?"

"Well, if I knew that, I wouldn't be here, would I?" She said it lightheartedly, but the words carried the frustrations she felt.

"No, I mean, it's a small town. You've likely been with most of these people since kindergarten, but after graduation you may never see many of them again. You get one opportunity to have them all as your captive audience before you all go your separate ways. What do you want to say to them before you do?"

Sadie thought about what he was saying. It was true that she had been with her class for the past thirteen years. It was also true that she likely wouldn't see many of them after this week. There was freedom in that thought. No longer would she be a slave to her past and others' perception of her. But although she didn't have deep relationships with many of her peers, there was a sadness that resonated, too. Everything and everyone that she has known was about to change. She was closing a chapter on her life.

"I guess I would want to acknowledge our history together but wish them well as they follow their own paths."

"Then do that," Tom prompted. "Listen, perfection is overrated. Trying to find exactly the right words you can drive yourself crazy. Just keep it simple and say what is on your heart."

Sadie chuckled and nodded. "That's what everyone keeps telling me."

"Then it must be good advice," Tom said. "Plus, if it's anything like my graduation most people won't remember it anyway." He shrugged and smiled a contagious smile.

"Gee, thanks," she responded sarcastically, slugging him on the shoulder.

"Hey!" He put his hands up defensively, laughing. "I told you I was going to be honest with you." Tom got up as if to leave. "It was nice to see you again, Sadie."

"Same." Sadie stood, too, hesitating for a moment before adding, "Graduation starts at 6:30 p.m. on Tuesday at the school gym. You know, if you wanted to come and make fun of those super attractive grad gowns."

Tom pretended to think about it for a moment and then said, "I would love to. And then maybe, once you have graduation behind you, you will let me take you out on a real date." His chocolate eyes glimmered with hopefulness and his crooked grin made her stomach flip flop. "Only this time maybe one without a room full of crazy middle schoolers."

Nodding, she had to agree. It would be nice to get to know Tom better, and it certainly would be easier without the addition of his youth group. "Deal."

"Friday night?"

Sadie mentally checked her calendar before agreeing. "It's a date."

Tom stuck his hands in his pockets and smiled at her. "I'll text you," he said as he turned to leave.

Sadie watched him walk away before she sat back down on the dock. She felt giddy. She felt excited. Most importantly, she felt inspired. Once she began to write, it was as if a dam broke, and words began spilling over the pages. She felt confident in her address to her peers. It wasn't perfect, but it felt honest. It felt like her. The more she worked on the speech, the more convinced she was that these were the thoughts she was meant to share with her class as she said goodbye to this season of her life.

CHAPTER SIX

"Do you have the camera?" Lynn asked Jack, slightly frantic as they rushed to get all three of them ready and out the door on time.

"Yes. It's right here." Jack held up a small camera bag. "Do you have the tickets?"

Lynn patted her purse. "Yes, I've got them. We are ready to head out."

Sadie chuckled at her loving family. "You do know that the graduation ceremony isn't due to start for another hour and a half, right?"

Jack scoffed and brushed the comment off with a wave of his hand. "Gotta beat the traffic," he said with a twinkle in his eye. Sadie rolled her eyes. The only traffic in this town was when a bunch of cars got stuck behind a tractor moving hay.

"We want to be sure to get good seats. This is a big day you know." Lynn paused and pulled a small, wrapped package out of her purse. "And we also wanted to make sure we had time to give you this." She pressed the package in Sadie's hand, giving it a squeeze as she did. Jack stood close and put his arm around his wife, the two of them smiling proudly at their niece.

"You already gave me a graduation present," Sadie said. "What's this?"

Jack chuckled. "You won't know unless you open it."

Sadie set down the grad gown and papers she held in her arms and sat on the bottom steps of the staircase. Gingerly, she ran a finger under the tape and tore off the metallic paper. She opened a small black box to reveal an oval locket on a delicate gold chain. Sadie held her breath. Using her thumbnail, she carefully opened the pendant to reveal two pictures—her mother and her father. They were both smiling. A lump lodged in Sadie's throat and tears filled her eyes.

Milestones were hard. Each one was a stark reminder of her parents' absence. Graduation was just one more thing that they were missing. One more memory made without them. It still hurt so deeply. A child does not get over losing their parents; they just get better at coping with the pain. No matter how much she processed and healed, grief was unpredictable and would hit her hardest unexpectedly. She would find a note they had written or catch a whiff of her dad's brand of aftershave on someone else and in those moments the pain would be almost unbearable. She would feel completely and utterly alone, questioning why she was spared and they were not. Other times she was able to remember them and smile at the memories. She would find herself daydreaming about what life would be like if they were still alive. So much of what she did was for them. She wanted to make them proud of who she became, of the life she was living. She wanted surviving to count for something.

The unpredictable nature of her grief would not take her by surprise today. Today was a day for which Sadie had prepared herself. Like a soldier bracing for a coming attack, she had mentally steeled herself against grief's arrows. Today she was saddened by their absence, but not crippled by it. Emotional, but not overwhelmed. The love and support that she had been gifted by Lynn and Jack was a blessing—and not one afforded to many orphaned children.

Lynn spoke, pulling Sadie's attention back to the moment. "You are a daughter to us. You know that, don't you? It has been our greatest honour to continue to guard and care for you and to finish that journey for my sister and her husband. We have loved watching you grow, and we could not be more proud of who you have become." Lynn looked Sadie directly in the eye and spoke intentionally, her voice filled with sincerity. "God has brought us joy in our pain. Tonight, we will be cheering you, immensely proud of the woman you have become, and we believe that your mom and dad will be watching and celebrating you, too."

The tears that had clung to Sadie's eyelids escaped and silently cascaded down her cheeks. She didn't try to stop them. The mourning was her way of paying tribute to her parents who loved her so dearly. Sadie ran a thumb over the locket and looked first at Lynn, then Jack. "Thank you. Thank you for this beautiful gift and loving me as if I were your own." Her heart ached for her parents, but as she looked down at their smiling faces inside the locket, Sadie felt close to them. Sometimes she was afraid of forgetting, but in this moment, their memory glowed brightly in her mind's eye. She fastened the dainty locket around her neck and wiped her cheeks.

Jack and Lynn drew Sadie into a loving embrace. They stood in the entryway like that, no one speaking, for several minutes before Jack broke the silence.

"Alright, well, I'd say that's enough emotional talk for one day. It's time to celebrate you, my dear. And I was serious about beating that traffic. I don't want anything to stand between me and a front row seat."

As soon as they arrived at the school, Sadie and her aunt and uncle parted ways. The graduates were to gather in the cafeteria with their teachers and other dignitaries. Sadie waved them off and laughed to herself as she watched Jack weaving through the crowd toward the front of the gymnasium with long, intentional strides—a man on a mission. Lynn was trailing behind him and speed walking so as not to get left in the dust. *Apparently, he wasn't kidding about a front row seat,* she thought.

The cafeteria was a bustle of activity as her classmates arrived. Teachers were moving through the room assisting students with their caps and gowns, ensuring that every tassel and sash was in place. Looking around the room, Sadie spotted Dawn. Her best friend was looking at her reflection in the glass of the door and attempting to adjust her grad cap so that it was straight. Sadie skipped over and squeezed her arm, making Dawn jump. She turned to face Sadie and squealed.

"You're here!" She pulled Sadie into a bear hug that knocked Dawn's grad cap to the floor. Dawn reached down to pick it up with a grumble. "Now you can help me get this stupid hat on. I don't know who invented them, but they definitely had zero fashion sense. I just can't get it on without my hair looking funky." She tried again without success and pouted at Sadie.

"Let me try," Sadie offered, taking the cap from her friend. Sadie placed the cap on Dawn's head and adjusted her long hair around it. "How's that?"

Dawn looked at her reflection from every angle. "I think it will work. Thanks. I just hope that no one sees me when I take it off. Talk about hat head!" Dawn switched her focus back to Sadie who was now donning her own cap and gown. "How are you feeling? Any nerves about giving your speech?"

Sadie took Dawn's place in front of the glass and wrestled her copper curls under the blue grad cap. It certainly was not a flattering look by any stretch, but it made the graduation feel official. Turning to face Dawn, she replied as honestly as she dared. "Yes, lots of nerves. I am happy with my speech, finally, but there were several times today I seriously considered skipping it all and going to the movies." She shrugged, "But, you know, it's our high school graduation. I'm told it's kind of a big deal."

"You think?" Dawn laughed. "Don't worry, you'll be amazing. But whatever you do, don't picture everyone in their underwear. My uncle gave me that advice for my grade seven piano recital." She shivered, "Let's just say that it was not helpful."

Then Dawn got a very mischievous look in her eyes. She looked side to side to ensure that no one was within earshot. "Did you bring the…" she paused, looking for the right word, "contraband?"

Sadie looked confused. "What are you talking about?" Dawn's schemes were not new to Sadie, but she usually had more information to go by.

"The contraband." Dawn lowered her voice to a whisper, looking side to side. "You know…the silly string."

Before exams, Dawn had discreetly spread the word throughout the grad class that they were to hide cans of silly string under their grad gowns on graduation night. Her plan was for everyone to "let the magic happen" at the end of the ceremony just as Principal Murphy declared them official graduates.

Sadie smacked her forehead, almost knocking off her cap. "No! I was so focused on remembering my speech that I completely forgot about it."

"Don't worry, girl, I've got you covered," Dawn whispered, reaching her hand into her gown and pulling out a small can of pink silly string. She discreetly handed it to Sadie.

"I do not want to know where you were hiding that," Sadie laughed. She simply couldn't help but be pulled along for the wild ride when Dawn was at the helm. No one could. Dawn's zest for life was contagious.

"My little secret," Dawn winked. "Okay, hide that quick. It's almost time to go."

Their banter was interrupted as Ms. Preston called for the attention of the class. Sadie slipped the can into the pocket of her sundress, grateful that dresses with pockets were in style. It was time to begin. Graduates were lined up alphabetically, so Dawn and Sadie gave each other a squeeze and parted ways, Dawn to the back of the line and Sadie to the middle between Dora Keller and Alex Lawson.

They could hear "Pomp and Circumstance" begin to play in the gymnasium as the procession began.

As she walked, Sadie spotted a familiar baseball cap. Tom was seated at the back of the auditorium smiling broadly. She caught his eye and gave him a little wave. Her heart responded to his presence by quickening its pace. *I can't believe he came. Or maybe I can.* Tom seemed to be a man of his word, and he had told her he would come. He had swapped out muck boots and flannel for dark wash jeans and a slightly wrinkled button-down shirt. Sadie appreciated the effort and thought he looked handsome.

The graduates filed into a section of reserved seats to the left of the stage. They were angled so that they could be seen by the audience but also were able to see the stage. It was sweltering in the gymnasium, and the heavy gowns weren't helping. Large fans were positioned throughout the crowd, but their effect was almost non-existent. Sadie could feel beads of perspiration forming on the back of her neck. She was grateful for the bottle of water that was placed under her seat. Around the room several people were fanning themselves dramatically with their programs. Sadie tried hard to focus on the speakers as they addressed the grads.

Before she knew it, Mr. Murphy was at the podium introducing Sadie. Taking a quick swig of water and grabbing the speech from under her chair, Sadie slowly made her way to the front of the stage. Standing at the podium, she paused a moment before she began, her eyes scanning the crowd. Her gaze rested on Jack and Lynn in the front row. Jack was hidden behind the camera, filming every moment. Lynn gave her an encouraging smile and a nod. She took a deep breath and began.

Good evening, ladies and gentlemen and fellow graduates. It is an honour to be standing before you as valedictorian. But if I am being honest with you, I struggled to write this speech. It is intimidating to think about standing in front of your peers, and your teachers, and your family, and being responsible for saying just the right thing to commemorate the time spent. To attempt to impart some sort of wisdom to inspire each of you to greatness.

For days I stared at a blank notebook. The pages taunting me in their empty potential and my inability to fill them. Then it hit me. We are just like that notebook. By trying to find the perfect words, I had silenced myself from saying anything. By trying to come up with exactly the right motivational quote to inspire you to be the best version of yourself, I found no words at all. This is a new chapter for each of us. Starting now, our futures are blank pages. If we become fixated on trying to find the perfect school, the perfect career, the perfect friends, the perfect boyfriend or girlfriend, then we risk experiencing any of it. We expose ourselves to the possibility of missing the good right in front of us if we are always searching for something better.

I know as well as anyone that life isn't perfect. In fact, most of the time it's a downright mess. But we cannot be so afraid of making the wrong choices that we do nothing at all. And when we mess up—notice I said when and not if—when we mess up, we cannot be afraid to try again. Failure doesn't mean that we are worthless; it simply means that we are one step closer to getting it right.

Thank you to our teachers, and families, and friends who stood by us and helped us learn how to make mistakes. Who taught us that it is okay to try again. Who taught us that life is about imperfectly loving imperfect people. As we step out into something new, something scary, something exciting and challenging and hard, may we remember that there isn't one right path for any of us. We simply need to do our best with the choices we make, and we need to love deeply the people who choose to do life alongside us. Thank you.

Returning to her seat, Sadie sighed with relief. The hard part was over. Now she could relax and enjoy the rest of the night. Dawn looked over her shoulder and gave Sadie a thumbs up. At least she had her friend's approval, and that was good enough for her.

The remainder of the ceremony was a blur. Tom was right in saying that it would be hard to remember much of it. There were several speeches from school staff and local dignitaries, but they all sounded the same. Diplomas were handed out and pictures were taken. Awards were handed out and more pictures were taken. Sadie won several awards, which was exciting but expected for someone who was at the top of her class. The grand finale, though, was something that Sadie would not soon forget. As the principal took to the podium and instructed them all to stand, the class members shifted and fidgeted as they reached into hidden compartments for their silly string. They moved their tassels from the right to the left, and just as the principal declared them graduates, Dawn let out the first whoop. Soon, multi-coloured streams coursed across the air like confetti. Sadie sprayed her silly string into the air and reveled in the childlike fun. She felt free. She wanted to freeze this moment and seal it away. This was the perfect tribute. This was how she wanted to remember high school—her classmates laughing, unified, having fun. Leave it to Dawn to make sure that the night would be memorable.

The graduates were instructed to head straight outside for group pictures. Family and friends were encouraged to join them out in the parking lot to offer congratulatory well wishes. When they were finished with the pictures, Sadie found Jack and Lynn standing off to the side waiting. Sadie quickened her pace and rushed to embrace them. First Jack and then Lynn. Lynn hugged Sadie for a bit longer than normal, savoring the moment and expressing her deep love for Sadie.

Lynn then held Sadie at arm's length by the shoulders and looked her at with glistening eyes. "We are so proud, honey," Lynn said. She smiled and pulled a clump of green and blue silly string from Sadie's hair. "Your speech was so well-done. I think you said exactly the right thing."

"Thank you, Auntie Lynn," Sadie responded. She then noticed Tom. He was leaning against the brick wall of the school and seemed to be having a lighthearted conversation with a younger boy holding a skateboard. The boy was laughing at something that Tom had said. "Oh, would you both excuse me for a minute. There's someone that I need to talk to."

Sadie headed in Tom's direction, discreetly checking to make sure that no other stray pieces of silly string remained lodged in her hair or on her face. Tom looked up and smiled when he noticed her walking toward him. He said something to "skateboard boy" and clapped him on the shoulder as the boy dropped the board and scooted away.

"Hey," Tom said as she stopped in front of him. He shoved his hands in his pockets and rocked on the balls of his feet.

"Hey," Sadie responded. "You came."

"I came," Tom said. They smiled at each other, their eyes locked in a gaze that allowed the silence to speak the words their lips weren't ready to confess. For a moment, Sadie felt the crowd and the noise fade until all she could hear was the beating of her heart.

The silence was broken by a bubbly brunette in wedged heels and a now multi-coloured grad cap. "Hi!" she said enthusiastically, sidling up to Sadie. "I'm Dawn Steeves, Sadie's best friend since, like, forever. We are practically joined at the hip. My mom calls her my sister from another mister. I wouldn't say that though because it's super cheesy, but I do think of her like a sister." Dawn wrapped an arm around Sadie protectively.

"I think he gets it," Sadie muttered through a clenched grin.

"I just wanted to make sure that he knew that if he's going to be sticking around that he will likely be seeing lots of me." Dawn explained.

Since it seemed unlikely that the ground would open up and provide a much-needed escape from the awkwardness, Sadie did her best to roll with it. "Tom, Dawn. Dawn, Tom."

Ever the gentleman, Tom remained unfazed and extended his hand to Dawn in greeting. "Nice to meet you Dawn, the sister from another mister."

Dawn giggled, shaking his hand. "Let's agree to forget I said that, okay? Glad you were able to make it." She turned to face Sadie. "I'm heading out. Mom doesn't want to miss our reservation at the House of Lam. Sleepover at my place tomorrow night?"

"You got it," Sadie agreed. "I'll text you." Her raised eyebrows indicating to her longtime friend that those three words carried the promise of sharing all the details of her encounter with Tom.

Dawn caught the hint and nodded seriously. "You'd better. Chat later."

With that, Hurricane Dawn left, leaving Tom and Sadie alone once again. "Dawn can be…" Sadie searched for the right word. "Enthusiastic, but she's right, we are best friends. We have been since preschool. I would never have survived without her."

"Having a friend like that is a gift. She seems like a lot of fun. I can't wait to get to know her. But," he paused, "don't sell yourself short. You would have found a way. You are strong—stronger than you realize."

Sadie felt the heat in her cheeks. *He is always so complimentary. Can he actually be serious or is he just feeding me a line?* "Thank you for saying that. I would like to believe that is true, but I'm not so sure."

"That's okay. I'm happy to keep trying to convince you. But it looks like that will need to wait for another time." Tom looked over Sadie's shoulder and gestured with his head to something behind her. Turning Sadie saw her aunt and uncle hovering just out of earshot, watching the two with interest.

Sadie gave them a wave and said reluctantly, "That's my aunt and uncle. Looks like it's time for me to go." For a moment the two stood awkwardly, neither sure of what to do next. Finally, Sadie reached and gave Tom's arm a squeeze. "I really appreciate you coming. I'll see you on Friday."

"I'm looking forward to it," Tom replied. And with that Sadie joined her family and headed home.

As Jack pulled their Civic into the driveway, Sadie noticed an unfamiliar car was parked on the street in front of their house. A middle-aged man sat in the driver's seat, and he was watching them closely. Immediately Sadie felt unsettled. An overactive imagination is helpful when you are reading and want to be transported to far-off lands, but it is not helpful when your mind starts playing out scenarios from episodes of unsolved mysteries. She searched the backseat of the car for something to use as a weapon if needed, but only managed to find McDonald's takeout trash. *Guess we are going to be at his mercy.*

"Do you see that guy?" She asked nervously. "What's he doing? Do you think that he is going to hurt us?"

"What? Why on earth would you jump to that conclusion, Sadie Elizabeth?" Aunt Lynn reprimanded. "He probably just wants to sell us something. Relax."

Jack nodded in agreement with his wife, but got out of the car, pulled himself to his full height and tried to look intimidating. It probably would have been more effective if his dress shirt didn't pull tight at his belly when he threw his shoulders back.

The man got out of the car, looking significantly less intimidating than Sadie had originally thought. She felt herself relax. He was no taller than her at five foot seven and he wore an ill-fitting blue suit. The suit jacket was unbuttoned and the white shirt underneath revealed what looked to be a mustard stain. The stain rested on top of a very rotund stomach that looked like it was familiar with the bottom of a burger box. In his right hand he carried a brown leather briefcase and with his left hand he adjusted the thick glasses perched on his pointed nose. No, he was not an intimidating man, but his eyes carried a look of intense determination.

"Mr. and Mrs. Russell?" The man questioned.

"Yes," Jack responded. "How can we help you?"

"My name is Detective Adams. I am here on a matter that concerns your niece." He gestured to Sadie. "Perhaps we can all go inside and talk for a moment privately?"

"Me?" Interjected Sadie. "What did I do?"

Lynn looked nervous. She placed a hand on Jack's arm as they exchanged an indiscernible look. Lynn took a deep breath and responded first. "Why don't we all go inside where it's comfortable, and we can hear what Mr. Adams has to say." She headed toward the house. Jack extended his arm indicating for Sadie and the detective to follow her as he brought up the rear.

Once inside, Lynn's hospitable nature took over as she went straight to the kitchen and began pouring glasses of lemonade. Jack sat in his armchair, and Detective Adams sat opposite him on the couch. In the corner of the room, Sadie stood, pacing and twisting her curls around her fingers—something she always did when she was nervous. *Who is this man, and what could he possibly want with me?* Jack seemed calm, but his stoic expression was unreadable, out of the norm for her naturally jovial father figure.

Lynn returned, balancing a tray with four glasses of lemonade which she offered to the detective first. He politely accepted the glass and placed it on a coaster on the table next to him. As Lynn handed out the rest, Detective Adams opened his briefcase and retrieved a thin yellow folder which he opened and laid in his lap.

He cleared his throat and began. "The matter at hand concerns the closed adoption of one Mr. Mark Burgess. He has hired me in his endeavours to uncover relevant information pertaining to the details of his birth."

Sadie stopped pacing and stared at the man waxing eloquent in the middle of her living room. "I'm sorry, but can you talk in words that we can understand? Who is this guy and what does he have to do with me?"

Detective Adams adjusted himself in his seat so that he was facing Sadie. He levelled his gaze and spoke simply, "Miss Jones, my client, Mr.Mark Burgess, has hired me to find his birth family. It appears that you are his closest living relative."

"Me?" She questioned.

"Yes, you. Miss Jones, you are his sister."

Chapter Seven

It took a moment before Sadie was able to regain her breath. The weight of his words were a sucker-punch to the gut. She slumped onto the couch, disbelief washing over her.

"I have a brother?" Sadie repeated, the words sounding absurd even as she said them. "How can that even be possible? I'm an only child. And an orphaned one at that." She looked to Lynn and Jack for backup on this. They both looked tense and strained, but they were not displaying the same level of shock that she felt.

"Being that it was a closed adoption, Mr. Burgess had very little knowledge of his birth other than the date and the fact that he was born in Lunenburg, Nova Scotia. It was not an easy task given the level of privacy that was requested, however, after some digging, I was able to trace his parentage back to your mother, Cora Jones."

Sadie was now completely confused. Her head was spinning. "I don't understand. Mom didn't have any other children. You have to be mistaken." She looked to Lynn and Jack for support. "Right? Auntie? Uncle Jack?"

Jack cleared his throat and suddenly looked very interested in the upholstery of his chair. Lynn pursed her lips. She moved to sit next to Sadie, taking Sadie's hands and holding them tightly in her own. Lynn had tears in her eyes as she spoke. "I wish that I could tell you that none of what this man is saying is true. Your mother was a wonderful woman. She loved you with an unshakeable love, but," her words caught in her throat, "there were things about her that you didn't know. Things that she had planned on telling you once you were old enough to understand."

Lynn took a long, deep breath as though trying to summon up courage to continue. "When we were teenagers, your mom and your grandmother did not have a healthy relationship. Our mom was very hard on Cora as the eldest child. She set strict rules and high expectations. When Cora was about sixteen, she got tired of it all and rebelled. Life for her became about doing things that would prove her independence from her parents' rule, which meant lots of parties, alcohol, and breaking curfew. More than once she asked me to cover for her as she slipped out our bedroom window in the night. I don't always know where she went or the specifics of what took place, but she would come back looking a mess."

Lynn paused, clearly struggling with sharing memories of Cora, especially ones that cast her in a negative light. "I was only fourteen at the time. I did my best to try and talk some sense into her, but she was too enmeshed in that world that it seemed impossible to quit. And then she started getting sick. At first, she thought it was the stomach flu, but after a week or so it became clear to all of us that she was pregnant."

Sadie gasped. She opened her mouth to speak, but there were no words. Like Alice and the rabbit hole, Sadie felt as though she were falling into a world of alternate realities, a world where everything she knew to be true was actually a deception.

Lynn looked to Jack for support. He nodded for her to continue with the story. "Cora was just a child herself, you see. She was in no position to raise a baby. The father was no better. He was a teenage alcoholic with little ability to care for even himself. We lost track of him, but I learned years later that he had died of a drug overdose. Mom and Dad were furious, as you can imagine, but once they calmed down, they were able to extend grace and mercy to Cora. It was a dark time for her, for us all, but it was the catalyst for change."

"It was decided that the baby would be put up for adoption. There was simply no other alternative at the time. Your mom was incredibly brave through it all. I cannot imagine the pain that she endured as she gave up her child without any hope of seeing him again. She was, of course, completely heartbroken. And that was about the time that she found Jesus." Lynn smiled as though lost in thought. "That's so often the way, isn't it? We have to hit rock bottom before we are able to see the lifeline that Jesus so graciously extends to us." She patted Sadie's hand.

"The recovery from that time was long and hard. Our family went to counselling to try and sort out some of the issues that had driven us to that point. Your mom missed a lot of school and ended up needing an extra semester to graduate. But in time, and through God's grace, we found healing."

The initial shock was beginning to settle leaving a minefield of questions in its wake. "Why has no one told me any of this before? Why all the secrets?"

Jack adjusted his position so that he was leaning forward, his elbows resting on his knees. "I know that this must be incredibly hard to process right now, but what you need to focus on is this—your mother loved you deeply and unconditionally. Considering what she had been through, there's no doubt that she loved you enough for two children. There were no secrets. There's a difference between secrecy and privacy. Cora kept the details of her past private because they were so painful to discuss. But it was our understanding that Mike and Cora intended on sharing this story with you themselves once you were old enough to truly understand."

Sadie refused to accept that as a justification. "But I'm old enough now. Why haven't either of you told me that I have a brother?" She looked back and forth between them.

Jack rubbed the back of his neck and said, "We spent a lot of time in the beginning discussing what we thought would be best. The honest truth is that we didn't want to tarnish the memory of your mother. It was a closed adoption. No contact between the two families. We assumed that the door was closed, and any further discussion of it would only bring you more pain."

"It is becoming clear that perhaps we made a terrible error in judgement by not telling you," Lynn interjected, "and for that we are so sorry, but please know that we did it with your wellbeing in mind."

Sadie's defenses softened at their explanation. It made sense that they would not see a need to tell her, but her mind was still reeling.

Frustration and anger began to bubble under the surface. How could her parents keep this from her and then not be around to pick up the pieces? How could Lynn and Jack not tell her?

Detective Adams cleared his throat. Sadie jumped. She had all but forgotten that he was still there. "Forgive me for interrupting, but there are some details that we still need to discuss."

"Our apologies," Jack responded. "By all means, please continue."

The detective ruffled through his paperwork before pulling out a small photograph. "This is a picture of Mr. Burgess." He said, handing it to Sadie. "As you can imagine, he was very distraught over the discovery that his birth parents had passed. He is, however, very interested in connecting with you when you feel ready. This is his contact information." Detective Adams passed her a single sheet of paper.

Sadie examined the photograph first. The picture was a cropped headshot of a good-looking man in his thirties. She could see the resemblance to her mother in his brown hair, dark eyes, and bright, wide smile. Next, she scanned the sheet of paper. It listed his birthdate, home address, phone number, and email address. Sadie was puzzled.

"Wait. Is this right? It says that he lives in England," she questioned.

"Yes, that's correct," he replied. "Mr. Burgess lives in a small town called Chipping Norton. He has lived there for most of his adult life, I believe. You will note on the bottom of the page that there are instructions on how to call him as well as a reminder that there is a four-hour time difference."

Sadie nodded, scanning the sheet again and doing her best to take it all in. "Do you know anything else about him?" She asked.

"Not much. I've only spoken with him a handful of times, and our communication has been primarily business related. I do know that he is married and has a daughter, but I'm afraid I don't know much else. Please do connect with him. He has been very determined to find you and will be awaiting your call." He stood, preparing to leave. "I'll be on my way now. My apologies for interrupting this lovely evening."

Jack walked Detective Adams to the door and held it open for him. The detective reached into his coat pocket and pulled out a business card which he handed to Jack. "In case you ever need to reach me." Jack took the card and shook the man's hand.

"Good evening, detective," he said, and closed the door behind him.

Jack stood at the door and looked at Sadie. She was still sitting on the couch, Lynn next to her, both quiet. No one seemed to know what to say. The silence which so often brought Sadie a sense of peace felt thick and suffocating. She needed space. She needed time to process this news.

"Sadie—" Lynn began.

Sadie cut her off. "Listen, I know that you both probably had my best interest at heart here. We can talk about it later, but if you don't mind, right now I just need to clear my head."

Lynn had tears silently sliding down her cheeks. She looked as though she wanted to stop Sadie, but Lynn remained seated and only nodded. Jack spoke for both of them. "We understand. We will be here when you're ready to talk," he said quietly.

Turning, Sadie headed out the front door suddenly feeling very alone.

Chapter Eight

"Okay so tell me again exactly what your brother said?" Dawn questioned through mouthfuls of popcorn. The two were sitting close, submerged beneath a thick cozy blanket in spite of the summer heat. Spread across the table in front of them was a junk food feast that would give a dentist nightmares. Dawn had supplied the popcorn, cans of ginger ale, and Cheetos, while Sadie had brought homemade brownies and Twizzlers. Their sleepover agenda had quickly switched from binge watching their favourite new TV drama to dishing about all the details on Sadie's encounter with Detective Adams, the details about her mother's past, and then, most recently, the long conversation she had with Mark Burgess early this morning.

"Man, it is still so crazy to hear someone call him my brother." Sadie shook her head in disbelief as she reached for a Twizzler. "I feel like I'm living in an alternate reality." She took a bite of licorice and curled her legs underneath her. Taking a deep breath Sadie recounted the phone conversation again for her best friend.

"He was really friendly. He has been married for six years and has a three-year-old named Lily—which I guess makes me an aunt."

Dawn interjected. "Aunt Sadie. I like it."

Sadie laughed. "He said that he moved to England right after university because of a job. He had wanted to take a chance at a great career that would let him experience a new culture. He works in marketing, I guess. Apparently, he never intended to stay, but after he fell in love and got married, England became his permanent home. He travels to London all the time for his work—how cool is that?" Dawn nodded in agreement. "Then he asked a lot of questions about me: what I like to do for fun, how graduation went, what it's like living here. I expected him to ask more about Mom and Dad, but he didn't."

"Did you bring it up?" Dawn asked as she washed a bite of cookie down with a slurp of ginger ale.

"No. I didn't really have a chance. Honestly, I'm not sure what I would have said anyway. But here's the part I didn't tell you." Sadie leaned in and paused dramatically. "He offered to pay for me to fly there and stay with them for a few weeks this summer. He said he wanted a chance to really get to know me. Can you believe that?"

Surprise registered on Dawn's face. She tapped a finger on her chin and responded, "Wanting to get to know you? Yes. Paying for a complete stranger to fly halfway around the world to live in your house for a few weeks? Not so much."

Sadie threw a handful of popcorn at her friend. "England is not halfway around the world you know. It's just across the ocean."

Dawn picked a piece of popcorn out of her hair and popped it into her mouth. "You know I suck at geography." She shrugged. "It may as well be on the other side of the world. So, what are you going to do? That's a pretty significant commitment for someone you don't even know. I mean, who's to say that he isn't a serial killer or something."

"Serial killers don't hire detectives to find their long-lost families and then pay tons of money to see them. Plus, Jack talked to Detective Adams again today to make sure that he was legit. I talked it over with my aunt and uncle, and we decided that this would be a good thing. I've got some time now before getting ready for school in the fall, so the timing works, and besides, it is really hard to pass up a free trip to Europe. You know it's always been my dream to go there."

"That is a good point. Do you think that he would consider flying me over, you know, for moral support? I've heard European men are incredibly romantic."

Sadie laughed until tears brimmed on her eyes. "Of course that's where your head is. You are the most boy crazy person that I know. How are you single right now? Not interested in Josh the goober?" Sadie said, remembering Dawn's prom date.

"Hey," Dawn said, defensively. "That goober turned out to be an incredibly sweet guy. But I can't be getting tied down with a relationship right now, I've got my sights set on college boys, and I plan on being a free agent." She sighed wistfully. "This is going to be a great fall."

From their hideaway in the basement, the girls heard the front door open, and Ms. Steeves call out that she was home. Moments later, they heard footsteps on the staircase that descended to the basement living space. Barb Steeves poked her head around the corner.

"Hi girls. What are you up to?" she asked.

"Hi, Mom," Dawn replied. "We're just eating enough sugar to make the oompa loompas jealous. How was work?"

Barb sighed and ran a hand over her face. "It was long. The ER was filled today. I don't know what was going on, but it meant that there were no breaks and my supper was a lukewarm cup of coffee I chugged between admissions." Barb often talked about how her job as an ER nurse was both exhausting and rewarding. She once told Sadie that she found a lot of purpose in helping calm the fears and meet the immediate needs of sick or injured patients who arrived each shift, but the health care system here was deeply flawed, and the waiting room was often backed up. Sometimes a person could wait for hours and hours before being seen. It was an exhausting job to be a health care worker.

Barb had had several conversations with Sadie about it as she made decisions on post-secondary education. Yes, the health care system was flawed, but in spite of that, it was an essential service. People needed health care. People deserved good health care. Good health care from practitioners who actually cared and were passionate about making a difference. The importance of that had been impressed upon Sadie during her brief hospital stay after the accident. Her care was delivered with compassion and gentleness. She wanted to be able to do the same. Being a nurse practitioner felt like a more attainable road than doctor and would be less likely to put her into a mountain of debt. She was anxious to get started this fall.

Before Barb could say anything else, loud plodding footsteps on the stairs announced the entrance of another interruption of their girlfriend share-fest. Dylan Steeves, Dawn's younger brother, ambled into the room looking more than a little disheveled. It was clear that he had already embraced the summer holidays and appeared to be fasting any form of personal hygiene. His gangly, fourteen-year-old body was dressed in an oversized, grey hoodie and Spiderman pajama pants. His shaggy, sandy blond hair stuck out in all directions, clearly using grease as a natural hair gel. Around his neck was a headset that attached to a gaming controller in his hands—a permanent fixture for Dylan during the summer months. But, perhaps the most humorous part of his ensemble were the giant, furry reindeer slippers that adorned his feet.

"There you are, Mom," he said. "I thought I heard you come in. Can we order pizza? I'm starving."

"You're always *starving*," Dawn mocked, adding extra emphasis to the word 'starving.'

Barb shook her head. "What about supper? Did you eat the food I left for you in the fridge?"

"Yeah, but that was like," he paused, counting in his head, "three hours ago."

With an exasperated sigh, Barb threw up her hands. "You'd think I worked just to support your appetite. Fine. Order a large though and share some with Dawn and Sadie."

Dylan suddenly became aware that there were others in the room. First, he noticed the girls, and then he noticed the food. "Hey, cookies. Sweet!" He reached to grab a cookie as Dawn chucked a throw pillow at his head. Expertly dodging the pillow, Dylan grabbed two cookies, which he immediately stuffed into his mouth before darting up the stairs.

"Ugh," Dawn huffed. "Can we ship *him* to England?"

Barb patted her daughter on the shoulder and smiled with a knowing look. "He won't always irritate you like this, but he will always be your brother. Try to have patience. And try to get to bed at a decent hour. Please? I'm going to go shower. I'll be upstairs if you need anything." Barb's words may have been directed at Dawn, but they stunned Sadie with their significance. Sadie had a brother. Certainly not likely to be one that played video games all day and wore reindeer slippers, but a brother nonetheless.

Once they were alone again, Dawn shifted gears. "Alright, so I doubt your newfound brother is going to open his pocketbook for his long-lost sister's BFF, which means that all my romantic daydreaming is going to come from you and Tom. So," she pointed a Twizzler in Sadie's face, "Dish."

For the next two hours, the two friends shared whispered stories, belly laughs, and future dreams. It was a kind of sacred space created by two hearts completely accepting and supporting one another. In Sadie's mind, it was exactly the way that all friendships should be—void of drama, judgement, and envy. Friendships had never come easy to Sadie. There were not countless people that she felt a deep, honest connection to, but she was so grateful for Dawn and the ability to be transparent and authentic with her. Dawn and the Steeves family were another one of those blessings in her life that Pastor Ted had talked about on Sunday—of that she was certain.

Chapter Nine

Two days later, Sadie still felt recharged emotionally after her night of sisterly bonding at Dawn's. Physically, though, her body had had a hard time recovering from the few measly hours of sleep that they had managed to fit in before Dawn had to be up and ready for her job at the local grocery store. In spite of the early morning, Dawn had been the instigator in their late-night antics, as was usually the case, arguing that the best sleepovers had very little to do with sleep. Just as Sadie had been ready to turn in to bed, Dawn decided that they simply *had* to watch a cheesy romantic comedy. Against her better judgement, Sadie agreed.

Sadie had spent most of Thursday at home in her PJs. The house had been empty since Lynn was out running errands and Jack was at work. It had been a glorious day of napping, reading, and napping some more. It felt luxurious to be able to enjoy a day of nothingness guilt-free—a welcome change from the last few months. Sadie reveled in the escape that her books offered. An intriguing romance novel mercifully kept her mind too occupied to focus on her own problems, of which there seemed to be a growing amount.

Mark had wasted no time in booking her flight to England. The paperwork arrived via email this morning. She would leave in just over a week. It all seemed incredibly surreal. Her mother's secret past, a half-brother, a trip to England. With so much to process, she opted not to. She was a pro at burying her problems. Tonight, she would go on her first real, official date with Tom, and she wanted to focus on that, and not the fact that her life as she knew it was unravelling.

Several outfits lay strewn across Sadie's bed, her closet ravaged. Tom was picking her up for their date in a half an hour, and she still could not decide on something to wear. Dawn had stopped by earlier and forced Sadie to model several outfits. They had agreed on cute and casual—dark wash jeans paired with a billowy, pale yellow top, but she was second guessing herself now. It didn't help that Tom was remaining mysterious about the details of the night. All she was able to discern from his cryptic texts was that they would be getting food and that she should bring a sweater in case the evening was cool.

Changing out of the outfit Dawn had selected, Sadie went back to the closet and finally settled on a blue floral print, A-line sundress. The tee shirt style of the dress made her feel comfortable, but it was still dressy enough in the event that they ended up somewhere classy. And it had pockets. In Sadie's opinion, all dresses should come with pockets. Digging into the mound of clothes on her bed, she retrieved a long, tan cardigan. It would pair well with the outfit and keep her warm if needed. Lastly, Sadie pulled her favourite white, canvas sneakers from the closet. She smiled as she slipped them on. *It may be a fashion faux pas, but at least I will feel like me,* she thought.

The doorbell rang promptly at 6 p.m., announcing Tom's arrival. Sadie grabbed her purse and darted for the door, but Jack intercepted her, holding up his hand. "A young lady should never answer the door herself," he said. "At least on the first date. Let your uncle give his approval." He smiled and gave her a wink.

Jack opened the door and welcomed Tom inside. "Good evenin' lad. You must be Tom," he said, extending his hand. "I'm Jack Russell, Sadie's uncle. Come on in. How she goin'?" Jack's South Shore accent was never more noticeable than when he was greeting someone. 'She' could refer to any person and often even inanimate objects. Sadie thought it was endearing and a testament to his deep Nova Scotia roots. Tom met Jack's hand with a hearty shake and stepped inside.

"The very best, sir. And yourself?"

"Oh, I can't complain, can't complain," Jack responded.

Seeing Tom made Sadie's palms clammy and her heart flutter like hummingbird wings. His head was absent of his trademark ball cap, allowing his wavy, boyish brown locks to fall where they desired. He wore a pale blue, long sleeved Henley shirt with the arms pushed up to his elbows, highlighting his perfectly toned arms. Light washed jeans and faded, black, sneakers completed his look. Tom's brown eyes sparkled with pleasure as he noticed Sadie on the stairs.

Smiling at each other, their gazes remained locked in a private moment until Jack cleared his throat. "Now seein' how Sadie's dad isn't with us, looks though it's going to fall to me to make sure you toe the line. Mind you, her dad was a real likeable guy, everybody thought so. Smile that could light up a room. I'm sure he would have let you off easy. But I'm a bit of a harder sell, so you treat her well, you hear me?" His words were gruff, but his tone was lighthearted. "She's pretty precious to us."

"Jack!" Sadie exclaimed as she swatted her uncle's arm, both mortified and touched by the act. He merely shrugged playfully.

"Of course, Mr. Russell," Tom replied sincerely, "I wouldn't dream of doing anything else."

"Call me Jack," he said. "Have fun you two."

Tom stepped to the side and offered for Sadie to exit first. As she walked past, he lightly placed his hand on the small of her back for a brief moment. His touch was electric. She quickened her pace so as not to be once again caught up in a moment with him. Tom sidled up to her and then reached around so he could open the door of his beat-up, red, pickup truck and offer her a hand up.

"I've got this," Sadie said with a smile. She placed a foot on the running board, grabbed hold of the door and hoisted herself gracefully up onto the seat in one fluid move.

"I guess you do," Tom replied, closing the door and jogging around to the driver side.

It was clear that the truck had seen better days, both inside and out. Tom had obviously tidied around the passenger seat, but trash, clothing, and other random junk filled the space in the back. *Okay,* Sadie thought, *not the tidiest, but at least he's put in an effort to clean.* As the truck grumbled to life and Tom's attention was on the road, Sadie allowed herself the opportunity to study his face. His wavy hair was blowing in the breeze of his rolled down window. She loved his hair and tried hard not to think about running her hands through it. His chocolate brown eyes were happy and open. They held none of the darkness and pain that Tom had so openly shared about that night with the teens. The openness of those eyes reminded Sadie of her father. Tom's strong jawline was freshly shaven and gave him more of a boyish look than when he sported a shadow of stubble. And his smile. Lips that were often twisted up in a crooked grin framed perfectly straight, white teeth. When he smiled *that way* at her, it was as though he was cautiously walking through the garden of her heart and pouring sunshine on the long-darkened corners. He made her feel hope in ways she hadn't felt before. She sighed.

"Sorry about the heat," Tom explained. "I've been meaning to get the air conditioner fixed."

She was grateful that he had interpreted her sigh as a comment on the temperature and not her secret assessment of him. "It's not a problem; I like it warm." Sadie readjusted her position so that she was leaning against the passenger door and facing Tom. "So, tell me Mr. Carter, where we are going? Your texts were pretty vague."

He laughed, "You don't really like surprises huh?"

"Surprises lately haven't been all that great. I prefer to know what I'm getting into."

"And I prefer the mystery," Tom replied as he navigated the narrow streets of town. "I guess we are just going to have to agree to disagree on this one."

Sadie folded her arms in mock protest at his refusal to give her any more information. She didn't have to protest long as Tom pulled into the parking lot of a fancy seafood restaurant. Sadie had eaten here only once before for a special occasion with Lynn and Jack. The establishment was in the downtown core where tourists flocked during peak seasons. From what she heard, it was always packed and getting a reservation on the weekends was nearly impossible. With its captivating view of the harbour and mouth-watering fresh seafood dishes, it was no wonder. As they walked toward the building Sadie nervously smoothed the front of her dress.

She wasn't underdressed, given the "everyone welcome" dining style of all restaurants downtown, but she was a little self-conscious about the idea of having a fancy dinner here as a first date. It felt a little stiff. She wanted to get to know Tom, but she wanted to get to know the real him, not one that felt he had to work hard to impress her. Any hesitations that Sadie felt were silenced by the thought that he must have pulled some strings to get a reservation for Friday night at such short notice. As Tom held the door open for her, she gave him a forced smile, suddenly unsure of herself and their evening together.

Tom took the lead as he walked up to speak with the hostess. "Pick up for Tom Carter, please."

Pick up? Sadie thought. *Oh, thank goodness.* She released a breath that she didn't realize she'd been holding. Maybe Tom had a better sense of a first date than she had given him credit for. *I just hope that he didn't order anything with mushrooms.*

Once she was seated back inside the truck, Tom handed her the hefty takeout bag. She still had no idea what to expect, but Sadie had relaxed and was doing her best to enjoy the adventure. Being the center of Tom's attention felt good, and she warmed at the thought that he had spent time planning the details of the night just for her. As he drove, they chatted amicably. Sadie asked Tom lots of questions about his family and interests, and she tried not to think about the delicious aroma that was filling the truck cab and making her mouth water.

He had lived in Halifax his whole life and was the youngest of three boys. His parents were still together and had a home on the outskirts of the city. Tom had liked living there, but he far preferred the smaller, more rural towns like Lunenburg. He had a chocolate Labrador Retriever named Gunner, who lived with him in the basement apartment at his uncle and aunt's house. What surprised Sadie the most was his interest in teaching.

"I thought you wanted to be a fisherman," she asked.

"Nah. I mean, it's good, honest work and I am enjoying it for now, but it isn't what I want to do with my life, you know. If I have learned anything from volunteering with the youth group, it is that I really love being a positive role model for those middle schoolers. Teaching them and influencing them would be pretty cool, I think." He shrugged, nonchalantly. "I often wonder if my school years would have been different if I had an older guy that took a serious interest in helping me make good decisions."

"I like that. I think you would be an amazing teacher. What would you teach?"

Tom looked at her and smiled before turning back to the road. He flipped the signal light on and turned onto a dirt road. "Thank you for not thinking that it's a ridiculous dream. I've brought it up once or twice with my family, and they all kind of thought I was joking. They think that I'm better off following in my uncle's footsteps and fishing for the rest of my life. You know, a blue-collar type." He readjusted his position so that one arm was resting on the open window and one was on the top of the steering wheel. "I get it. I was never the strongest student, so I mean it is a little crazy that I feel drawn back to school. It's an unlikely career choice for me, but I was thinking that I might like to teach history."

"Really?" Sadie questioned.

"Yeah. It's a subject that just makes sense to me. There's something deeply satisfying about studying the past so that we can better understand our present and make better decisions in the future. And I like the idea about honouring the people whose stories we have documented. I would hope to make their lives count for something."

"That's really beautiful," she said. Sadie was a little shocked at his depth. The more she learned about Tom, the more he surprised her. He was certainly more than a jock bumming away a year on a fishing boat.

Tom's cheeks flushed. "Sorry. That was a little over the top, wasn't it?"

"Not at all. In fact, I'm impressed. I'm impressed that you have put so much thought into your future, and I'm impressed at your perspective on history." Sadie scrunched up her nose. "It's probably been my least favourite subject. Just way too much memorization. But maybe if I had had a teacher like you, it would have been different."

They had been driving for about ten minutes down narrow, wooded roads to a part of town that was unfamiliar to Sadie. Tom slowed down the truck, eased it onto a wide part of the road's shoulder, and turned the engine off. Instead of getting out of the truck he turned so that he was facing Sadie. "You know you are the first person that I've explained that to. I always have felt silly trying to get my family to understand. Thank you for being a good listener."

Now it was Sadie's turn to blush. Thankfully, Tom was now focused on food. Hopping out of the truck, he jogged around to her side, took the bag of food, and offered her a hand down. "Uhh," she said, taking in their surroundings, "I know you're hungry, but I'd venture that the wildlife in these woods are too. Are you sure this is where you want to eat?"

"Oh, we're not eating here," he said with a smile. "I just didn't want to park too close and give away the surprise." With the bag of food in one hand, Tom reached for Sadie's with the other. She allowed her small hand to be enclosed in his. It felt nice.

As they turned the corner, the tree line opened to reveal a wide channel of water lapping along a sandy shore. There was a short dock and parked at it was a fishing boat, presumably that belonging to Tom's uncle. At the back of the boat, facing out to the ocean, Tom had spread a blue checkered blanket. A small bouquet of purple tulips sat in a glass vase on the corner of the blanket and Christmas lights were strung around the boat's railing. Once the sun started to set, the rays would provide a soft light in the darkness.

"This way milady," Tom said guiding her toward the boat. Placing one foot on the edge of the boat and one on the dock, Tom offered Sadie his hand to help her onboard. This time she accepted his offer, not wanting to end up taking a dunk in the water. Tom hopped on board after her, still toting their hefty bag of take out, and took a seat on the blanket. Sadie sat on the blanket opposite him. Tucking her skirt underneath her, she stretched out her legs and crossed her ankles.

"This is fantastic. Thank you for doing all this," Sadie said.

"You're welcome. Sorry for the fishy smell. I did clean up, but I think that smell is permanent." Tom began unpacking the bag of food from the takeout bag and arranging it in front of her.

"How many people are you planning to feed with that," Sadie questioned. There was enough food spread out in front of her to feed three couples.

"I like to have options," Tom responded honestly. "And I like to eat. Okay, so you get first pick. We've got fish and chips, a lobster roll, a cheeseburger, some sweet potato fries, and a small poutine. What'll ya have?"

Sadie laughed. "Seriously Tom. Who is going to eat all that?"

He shrugged. "I was hungry, and I wasn't sure what you liked."

"Alright, I guess I'll have the lobster roll and the poutine."

"Great choices," he said, handing them to her. "And to drink we have water or Sprite." He reached into a cooler that was tucked in the corner and held up both options.

"Water, please," she said.

As they dug into the food, Sadie felt content. Being with Tom was easy. She didn't feel like there were expectations on how she needed to act, and that put her at ease. They munched contentedly on the delicious food and listened to the waves lap at the sides of the boat as they took in the beauty of their surroundings. The landscape around them was commonplace for those local to Lunenburg, but it still had the power to take Sadie's breath away. A seemingly infinite and rugged, deep green forest spread wide across the hilly land. Briny air filled their nostrils as a heron plodded its way along the shore in search of its own supper.

Finishing his burger, Tom crumpled the paper in his hands and reached for the fries. "Okay, Sadie Jones, I would really love to get to know you. In your own words. Not someone else's words. What has made you, you?" He paused. "If you're comfortable sharing it, that is."

Sadie contemplated his offer. It was a terrifying thought to embrace vulnerability, but she wanted Tom to know. She wanted him to know her. And so, as the Sun's golden orb melted into the ocean, Tom listened as Sadie shared her story. She told him about the night of the crash and about waking up in the hospital. She talked about life with Lynn and Jack and her frustrations with living in a small town where everyone knew her past and treated her as something fragile, something not quite whole. She told him about Detective Adams and discovering she had a brother. And then, because it felt so freeing to finally talk about it all and because Tom seemed to listen without judgement or self-pity, she told him of her deep anger at God.

There was no condemnation. No resentment or pious retort. Tom, in an outpouring of mercy, simply listened. Then he stretched out on his back on the blanket and stared up into the sky. The setting sun was creating a symphony of colour across the clouds. Reflected across the water were brilliant reds and yellows as if the waves wished to join in the song.

After several moments of quiet, he said softly, "You know, it wasn't supposed to be this way."

Sadie leaned back on her arms so she could look up at the sky too. "What do you mean?"

"When God created the world, he never intended for it to turn into such a mess. But we are messy. People are messy. And selfish, and arrogant, and lustful, and a whole lot of other things. I believe a lot of the time life is hard simply because our world is just broken. It's a cheap knockoff compared to the one God had originally planned."

Sadie absorbed his words and allowed them to rattle around. "Okay sure—but isn't God all-powerful? You were the one who said He can split the sea and cause the sun to stop. If the world is such a mess, why doesn't He do something about it?"

Tom thought for a moment before continuing. "I mean, He did. He sent Jesus to offer us a way out of our fate. Through Jesus we have a means of getting to the life that is the real deal. The perfect world God always intended."

It wasn't enough. Even with Tom's explanation, she simply could not accept that if God was loving—if He truly loved her—that He would allow her, or anyone else, to endure such misery. Grief and shame had long been Sadie's companions. Betrayal had newly joined them as she learned of her mother's past. It was from those deep wells of pain that she found her motivation in life, and in that, her identity. She wasn't ready to let them go on a whim to follow Tom and his beliefs only to be vulnerable to more pain. And she certainly wasn't interested in following a God who made his people endure such pain at the promise of an alleged pot of gold at the end of the rainbow. No, the walls she had built around her heart kept her safe.

Sadie shook her head. "I'm sorry, Tom. I know that you believe this, and I want to be able to say that I do, too. But I just can't accept that as justification for allowing us to deal with the misery of this world. I'm not interested in a personal anything with that kind of god."

"Just come with me to church on Sunday. I know that Pastor Jay will be able to explain this so much better than I can," he pleaded.

"It won't make a difference. And honestly, I'm not interested in changing my mind on this one." She looked at him intently. "Why do you care so much anyway?"

Tom pushed himself into a sitting position and turned so that he was looking at Sadie again. Reaching across the space between them, he took her hand in his and then he looked into her eyes and spoke with intentionality. "Sadie, I'm not going to tell you how you should feel, and I am not going to pretend that I understand what you have been through. It's just…" He looked up at the sky and rubbed the back of his neck. He seemed to be grasping for words.

"It's just that I really like you, Sadie. You're thoughtful, and interesting, and funny, and compassionate. But it's not fair to keep trying to convince you to see something you aren't willing to see. I still would like to be your friend, but I can't let my heart get romantically involved with someone who is completely shut off to Jesus. It just wouldn't work." His eyes looked pained as he spoke the words.

Sadie recoiled as though she had just been burned. In essence, she had. He had pursued her. He had asked her to be open and honest with him. How dare he plan this whole night, and let her share her most vulnerable self, only to get self-righteous. Her personal beliefs were none of his business. A mix of anger, embarrassment, and shame bubbled up inside of her.

"Fine." Sadie all but spit the word at him. "If that's how you feel, then I will take my sinful self and leave." She stomped off the boat onto the dock ready to make a dramatic exit before remembering that they were far from town and there was only one vehicle.

"Sadie, wait. Let me explain," Tom called after her. She stopped but kept her back to him. Hot tears filled her eyes, but her anger ordered them not to fall. Instead of succumbing to the hurt, she pulled her cardigan tight around her body, physically and emotionally shutting him out. Building walls was her defense mechanism of choice to help combat the emotions that too often threatened to overwhelm her. "What could you possibly have to say, Tom?"

He caught up to her and turned her around. "I'm sorry. I'm so sorry. This is all coming out wrong. I never meant to hurt you, I just..." His voice trailed off as he tried to make eye contact. Sadie stared at the ground, refusing to let him see any weakness. "I just can't let this be a big obstacle in our path. It would be leading you on to continue dating if we are never going to be able to agree. I don't want to hurt you."

"Yeah, well, it's too late for that," Sadie retorted. "I'd like you to take me home now."

Tom hung his head and relented. They drove back to Sadie's home in silence. Lynn was waiting up for her in the sitting room, knitting needles in her lap.

"How was your night, honey?"

"It turns out he wasn't the guy that I thought he was."

"Do you want to talk about it?" Lynn put down her knitting to give Sadie her full attention.

"No. I'm pretty beat. I'm just going to head to bed."

"I'm always here if you need anything."

"I know Auntie. Love you."

"Love you, too, honey."

Sadie mounted the stairs to her room, pausing to touch her fingers to the framed picture of her parents. "I miss you both so much," she whispered, the tears finally escaping. "I just really wish you were here."

In the privacy of her room, Sadie collapsed on the bed, burying her head in her pillow, and allowed herself to fall apart. All the anger that she had felt earlier melted away leaving a familiar deep, searing grief. Silent tears grew into deep sobs that shook her body and left her gasping for breath. She wept over Tom and the hurt that he had caused her. She wept for the years of feeling broken and abandoned. And for the first time in a long time, she wept for her parents.

When there were no tears left to cry, exhausted, Sadie fell into a restless sleep.

Chapter Ten

A very perky flight attendant pushed a beverage cart down the narrow aisle of the aircraft. Sadie dropped her tray table and readjusted her position in anticipation. A cold drink would feel nice right about now. They had been flying for almost four hours, and Sadie was parched. Her tongue was dry, and her teeth felt annoyingly fuzzy. She wished she had remembered to put a toothbrush in her carry-on bag. Even though she was flying a red-eye, sleep had eluded her. Her brain was on overdrive—it had been for days. She hadn't spoken with Tom since the night of their date, but that didn't mean that she had been able to put him out of her mind. Between managing the pain of his rejection and her anxieties over meeting her brother, Sadie was bringing with her more emotional baggage than the actual baggage she had stowed in the plane's cargo hold.

Initially, Sadie had been grateful for the window seat as it meant she'd be able to have a front row seat as night tucked the sun to sleep. However, it would have been nice to have the option to get up and stretch. The person sitting next to her had fallen asleep an hour ago, and she couldn't bring herself to wake the older gentleman to excuse herself. She did her best to stretch her legs in the cramped space and settled in.

As the flight attendant passed, Sadie gratefully accepted a glass of ginger ale and a package of airline cookies, which she balanced precariously on the tray as she popped her headphones into her ears. If she couldn't sleep, she might as well watch a movie. The aircraft was equipped with small, personal screens on the back of the seats, which offered each passenger in the next row a selection of movies and television shows to pass the time. Sadie selected a cheesy romantic comedy and adjusted the travel pillow around her neck. The movie was mindless, and about an hour into it, she found herself nodding off. Not wanting to fall asleep on her neighbour's shoulder, she shut the screen off, propped her head against the window, and closed her eyes.

An announcement from the captain startled her awake from a strange dream. They were beginning their descent, so trays needed to be stowed and seats needed to be moved out of the reclined position. Sadie was impressed that she had managed to catch a couple hours' rest, however poor it had been.

Disembarking took only a few minutes, but the close quarters and lack of airflow made it feel like hours. Sadie entered the terminal and inhaled a deep breath of fresh air—she had made it. Readjusting her backpack, she checked her purse to make sure her passport and wallet were still safely tucked into one of the pockets. She then set off to find a restroom as she made her way to the baggage claim area. Looking around, Sadie tried not to be overwhelmed. This airport made Halifax International look like a child's play set. She had travelled through airports before, but never alone and never one of such expanse. Following the flow of traffic from her plane seemed like a wise decision. As she walked, she kept a lookout for a restroom but saw nothing. Finally, the need became pressing enough that she found an airline attendant at an empty kiosk and asked for directions. The kind lady pointed to the wall directly behind her which read "W/C."

"WC?" Sadie questioned.

"Water closet. The restroom."

"Ah. Yes, thank you." Sadie was beginning to realize that there may be a bit of a learning curve on this adventure. She took her time in the rest area and did her best in the small sinks to freshen up. It was a lost cause. Her outward appearance seemed to be mirroring her emotional state. She looked a mess. Sadie wished again that she had thought to pack a toothbrush or even chewing gum in her carry-on bag. *Oh, well,* she thought, taking in her appearance in the bathroom's full-length mirror. *This is as good as it gets.* Her new family was going to get to meet her in all her airplane-jetlag-day-old clothes and bad breath glory.

After picking up her suitcase from the baggage claim, nervous butterflies awakened in the pit of her stomach. In just minutes, she would be meeting her half-brother. Would he like her? Would she like him? What was his family like? Would he be angry that he was put up for adoption? These questions and more swirled through her mind causing her to perspire nervously. *So much for freshening up,* she thought as she dried her palms on her sweatpants.

Taking a deep breath, Sadie steeled herself for the next step and walked through the exit doors and into the arrivals terminal. Dozens of people were standing waiting for their loved ones to arrive. She froze and scanned the large crowd, immediately regretting that she hadn't made more specific plans with Mark. Sadie reached for the phone in her purse to double check if there were any notifications, knowing full well that she had turned off her data until she knew for sure that it wasn't going to cost her a fortune.

Just as she was about to break into full-blown panic at the thought of being stranded alone in a foreign country, she mercifully heard someone calling her name. Sadie looked up to see a tall, lean man who strongly resembled her mother weaving through the crowd in her direction. The sunglasses atop of his short, dark brown hair were a testament to the sunshine of the mid-day and he was dressed in business casual wear. A white and blue printed dress shirt was tucked into crisply pressed black dress pants and he looked as though he had just left an important work meeting. All that was missing was a briefcase. She met him halfway and the two exchanged a slightly awkward hug.

"Sorry about that," Mark said. "I got held up at work and then the parking here is a nightmare. I hope you had a good flight. Let me officially introduce myself. I'm Mark." He paused, stepped back, and took a good long look at her.

"Sadie," she replied, extending a hand which Mark met with a warm shake. "Nice to officially meet you."

"It is such a blessing to have you here, Sadie. You can't begin to know how long I have waited to meet some of my birth family. We have so much to talk about, but I imagine you are just about ready to crash. Let's get out of here." He reached to take her suitcase and led the way out of the airport terminal to the parking lot.

Sadie was surprised to see that the sun was not shining as brilliantly as Mark's sunglasses suggested. In fact, the day was overcast and gloomy. Sadie imagined that the clouds were graciously keeping the sun at bay as an invitation for her to crawl under the covers and sleep the day away.

"This is us," Mark said, gesturing to a compact, blue car. "You hop in, I'm just going to put your suitcase in the boot."

"The boot?"

Mark laughed, "Yes. It's what we call the trunk here." He opened the *boot*, which was much smaller than she would have expected. Grateful that she had packed light, Sadie walked around to the passenger side, opened the door, and was about to slide in when she noticed the steering wheel.

"Oh!" She exclaimed. "I forgot about that."

"Yes," Mark said with mirth in his eyes. "I mean, you're welcome to drive, but I doubt it would be a wise way to start off your first visit to England."

Sadie held up her hands. "No, no. I'm very happy to be a passenger on this one." She walked around the car and slid into what should have been the driver's side. It was the strangest feeling. As it turned out, driving on the opposite side of the road is a nerve-wracking experience when you aren't used to it. Sadie white-knuckled the whole trip, feeling as though each oncoming vehicle was a missile aimed directly at her.

The sights outside the window provided a welcome distraction from the road. Sadie did her best to drink it all in as Mark kept the conversation light. He told her about his wife, Bridget, and his daughter, Lily. Bridget was born and raised in Oxford. The two of them had met while he was working as an intern at a successful marketing firm in the city. They dated for two years before marrying; Lily arrived two more years after that. Lily was, in her father's opinion, the most brilliant three-year-old on the planet. They had moved from their small flat in Oxford to Chipping Norton just after Lily was born because it was a smaller town and a nicer place to raise a family. Mark worked from home as often as he could and commuted to London or Oxford when it was required. The way he spoke made Sadie certain that family was his priority in life. He did not come across as a businessman intent on bulldozing through the company to the highest position at the expense of those important relationships. Instead, it seemed as though his work was fulfilling, but only inasmuch as it provided him with the freedom to be flexible with his schedule.

The vistas before them began to expand as they exited the metropolis of London and began driving through the countryside. Mark switched gears and excitedly donned the cap of tour guide, describing in detail the cities they were passing. Outside her window were sprawling farmlands and rolling hills. In many ways it was similar to Nova Scotia, except that thick forests were replaced with grassy plains and roadside drainage ditches were replaced with the occasional low stone wall.

"Welcome to the town of Chipping Norton," Mark declared enthusiastically. "The most beautiful Cotswold town in Oxfordshire—at least in my opinion."

Sadie had to admit, it was charming.

As they entered the city, rows of compact, tan-coloured brick townhouses lined the narrow street. Mark expertly navigated the car through the morning traffic as Sadie held her breath each time they met an oncoming car. She was certain that they would collide, but there was always just barely enough space for clear passage. After several minutes, Mark turned the car into a tiny driveway of one of the homes. It was quaint and simple and much less ostentatious than those Sadie was used to. The muted tans and browns of the town were a stark contrast to the multi-coloured buildings of Lunenburg.

A towheaded ball of pink bounded out of the front door and flung herself into the waiting arms of Mark.

"Daddy!" She screamed delightedly. Jubilant giggles bubbled up out of the little girl as her dad threw her up over his head and then tickled her belly. He set her on the ground and then crouched to her eye level.

"Lily, there's someone very important that I would like you to meet. This is Sadie. She is our family from Canada." Lily suddenly became bashful and tucked herself behind her father's legs. Sadie opened her backpack and reached inside. Aunt Lynn had been wise enough to suggest that Sadie bring along a little present for her new niece. She pulled out a small, stuffed moose with orange antlers and, following Mark's lead, crouched to Lily's level.

"Hi Lily. It's so nice to meet you. This is my friend Morris." She held up the stuffed animal. "He's a moose, and he just flew a really long way. He's pretty tired and could use a friend to take care of him. Would you like to be his friend?"

Cautiously, Lily crept out from behind her father's legs. She smiled and nodded. Taking the moose from Sadie, Lily cradled him in her arms and then squished him up to her cherub face. "Oh, I love you, Morris. I'm going to take very good care of you," she said and then tackled Sadie into a toddler-sized hug before skipping off to show her mother who had joined them outside.

Between her British accent and her inability to clearly enunciate the letters *L* and *R*, it may have been the most darling sentence Sadie had ever heard. She stood and saw that an adult version of Lily was now standing next to Mark.

"Well, you've clearly won her over. And Sadie, this is my lovely wife, Bridget," Mark said in introduction.

Bridget stepped forward and offered Sadie a gentle embrace. "It is so nice to finally meet you, Sadie. We have been searching for so long for Mark's family and are thrilled to welcome you into our home. What a brave thing that you have done coming here."

A lump lodged in her throat. She didn't feel brave. She felt like a coward running away from her problems. But she was here now, and she was ready to put all of that out of her mind. Bridget's simple and sincere manner immediately helped to put her at ease. Her accent made her sound elegant and regal, but her demeanour was open and kind. Bridget was tall with a slender frame. Her long hair hung well past her shoulders and the light blonde colouring mirrored her daughters. Bright blue eyes were framed by a heart-shaped face, and they wore an expression of tenderness to which Sadie felt drawn. Bridget was naturally beautiful, but there was something other than her appearance that gave her an attractiveness. Sadie was certain that they would be fast friends.

"Thank you so much for saying so," Sadie responded as honestly as she could. "And thank you both for bringing me here. It's always been a dream of mine to come to Europe."

Bridget responded. "As it should be. Our country is brimming with rich history and culture." She smiled knowingly before adding, "and good food. But enough of standing out here. You'll learn about all of that in due time; you must be exhausted. Let's get you in and settled so you can freshen up." With that she ushered them all inside the quaint townhouse.

Sadie started to take her shoes off at the door, but Mark stopped her. "Oh. Don't worry about that. In England, it is customary for people to leave their shoes on in the home." Looking at their feet, she realized that they had all left theirs on. Sadie, who often spent her days at home barefoot regardless of the season, wasn't sure that she was going to be a fan of that, but she complied anyway to be courteous.

The Burgess' home was small but cozy—and tastefully decorated. Immediately inside the front door was a staircase that led to the second story. To the right was a small sitting room filled with a grey sofa and two armchairs. Bookcases lined one wall and housed an expansive collection of literature that Sadie was anxious to explore. Beyond the staircase and opposite the living room, were three doorways. One led to a tiny guest room, one to a bathroom, and one to the kitchen.

"This will be your room here on the main floor. Our bedroom and Lily's are upstairs. I know that there isn't much space," Bridget said apologetically as she showed Sadie the room, "but, when it's not in use, you can stow the bed by lifting here." She grabbed the foot of the bed and hoisted it against the wall. It disappeared leaving an open space. Sadie was impressed. She had heard of Murphy beds but had never seen one before. *I just hope that it doesn't do that while I'm in it,* she thought.

Bridget led her into the kitchen where Lily was perched at a small circular dining room table in the corner. She was holding Morris the moose and appeared to be introducing him to a bright pink unicorn. The kitchen, like the rest of the house, was compact. Each space was being used efficiently and with minimal clutter. The refrigerator was not much bigger than a bar fridge and there was no freezer. In the place where Sadie would have expected a dishwasher was a washing machine, but no dryer.

Mark noticed her confusion. "Quite a bit different than the kitchens you're used to, huh? You'll notice that spaces aren't sprawling in the same way as back in Canada. Compact and efficient is key. Plus, people are more apt to buy groceries daily or as needed rather than stock up for long periods of time."

"Fascinating," Sadie said. "I'm sure that must have been an adjustment for you."

"There are lots of adjustments when you move to a new country, but I love it here. You'll get used to it all, you'll see." He began pulling items out of the cupboards. "Now, are you hungry? I can whip you up something to eat."

"Thank you, but I think I'm okay for now. They fed us lunch on the plane. I think I'm just going to stretch out for a few minutes."

"Alright, well, just let me know when you're ready to eat or, better still, make yourself at home here. But I do caution you that the best way to combat jet lag is to stay awake and sleep when we do."

"He's right, unfortunately," Bridget agreed. "And, please, do make yourself at home. If there is anything that you cannot find, do not hesitate to ask."

Mark added, "I left my travel wall adapter on the nightstand in case you didn't have one. It's what I use when I travel back to Ontario, so it has the Canadian outlet attachment."

"That's perfect; I never thought to bring one. Thank you all for your hospitality," Sadie mentally chided herself for such an obvious oversight as she headed to her guest room and flopped on the bed. Every muscle in her body was weary and begging for her to succumb to the exhaustion. Dreamland beckoned as she laid there for a moment contemplating what she should do first when she heard a knock on the door. Forcing her sleep-deprived body out of bed, she opened the door. Mark stood with an armful of linens.

"Sorry to disturb you, but I've got some towels for you. There's a linen closet with more in the hallway if you need them."

"This is great. Thanks so much," Sadie replied.

Mark started to leave and then turned back and added, "Listen. Take all the time that you need to recover from the trip. But once you are feeling up to it, I really am looking forward to talking with you. Bridget has planned some fun touristy outings for you, too. We are really happy that you are here."

"You are both so kind. I am sure I will be ready to take it all on once I catch up to my body."

She gratefully took the towels and closed the door. The truth was that Sadie was a little tentative about talking with Mark. What kind of information would he want to know about her mom? Would he want answers about his adoption—answers she didn't have? Would he force her to relive the painful memory of the accident? And yet, she had agreed to come all this way. Why? Part of it was curiosity. Part of it was that it offered an easy escape from the stress and drama of life back home. A big part of it was the inability to pass up a free trip to England. But more than any of those things, Sadie could relate to Mark. He had lost his connection to his birth parents a lot younger than she. Perhaps Sadie might finally have someone in her life who could understand the burden of grief she carried.

Chapter Eleven

Sadie sat on the edge of the bed as a battle of wills took place in her mind. Part of her wanted to lay back down and let her weary body nap. The other part was confident that her anxiety over talking to Mark wouldn't allow her to relax anyway so she should be productive. The latter won out, so Sadie grabbed a towel and trucked off to have a shower, thankful that the bathroom plumbing seemed to work the same as that back home.

Feeling clean and refreshed, Sadie stretched out on the bed to check if there were any messages from home. She had messaged back and forth with Lynn briefly when she first landed, but it had been very early morning. It was just like Lynn to be up waiting to hear that she was safe. It was almost lunchtime back in Lunenburg now, and so she sent them an update that she was finally settled at Mark and Bridget's home. Immediately the three little dots appeared to indicate that Aunt Lynn was responding. It read: "I'm so glad to hear that. Soak up the moments, Sweetheart. We love you."

Sadie smiled. She was so grateful that they had been able to talk through some of their issues before she left. They had apologized profusely for the secrecy, and their sincerity had dissolved any lingering anger that she harboured toward them. Regardless of how she felt about the situation, they were not malicious people, and their intentions in keeping her mother's secret, however misguided, had been in her best interests. Sadie knew that the hurt she felt wouldn't easily dissipate, but at least she was able to see their side of things.

She sent a heart and a hug emoji and rolled on her back, staring at the ceiling.

What a crazy turn of events. Just a few weeks ago she had been worried only about exams and prom. Now here she was on the other side of the world, as Dawn would say, spending time with her half-brother. Her heart had truly been on a rollercoaster ride, and Mark's entrance into her world had only been part of the cause. Unfortunately, not all her relationships had been mended. She pulled up a picture on her phone that she had been unable to bring herself to delete. It was one that she had snapped of Tom at the bowling alley, at Dawn's request, so that she could show him off to her friend. He's not looking at the camera, but he's laughing at something one of the middle school boys said as he stepped up to bowl. It was that happy, open expression that had made her fall for him so quickly.

A solitary tear escaped and slid down her cheek as she thought about the pain that he had caused her. Her phone had blown up with apology texts from Tom for a week after that awful night. He said that he was wrong for how he had hurt her. He said that he wasn't trying to be judgmental. He told her that he wanted another chance to talk, to explain. But it was too late; talking would only make things worse. He had made it clear that she wasn't good enough for him. She could never be. No matter how hard she had tried in her life she was never going to be anything more than a wounded bird doing its best to learn to fly without its mama and papa.

There was a part of her that wanted to believe everything that Tom and Pastor Ted and Lynn and Jack believed—that God was loving and wanted the best for His people. There had been moments she thought that maybe she could believe that God loved her and would enable her to move forward, but unlike Lynn and Jack, she couldn't find the strength or willingness to trust Him with her grief. She was not interested in a self-righteous religion that shut out the ones she cared about. It was simply too much for her to accept that God was a being whom she could trust enough to surrender her life. He took her parents and left her alone to pick up the pieces. She had not responded to any of Tom's messages, and eventually, they stopped; the absence of his messages made her feel both relieved and heartbroken.

Closing her eyes, Sadie forced herself to forget about Tom and soon drifted off into a deep sleep.

When she woke hours later, it took several minutes for her to regain her bearings. It came back to her in waves as her eyes adjusted to the dark room. *I'm in England. I'm actually here!* She looked at her phone. It was almost 11 p.m. in England, and in spite of the time, Sadie felt giddy. Getting up to go to the washroom she grabbed her phone to use as a flashlight. The house was quiet, so she did her best to make the trip as noiseless as possible.

Slipping back into bed, Sadie willed herself to go back to sleep, but her brain was not cooperating. She felt wide awake, and her stomach protested audibly. The airline meal was long gone. It seemed that she was going to have to scour for sustenance in the dark in an unfamiliar home. Huffing, Sadie rolled out of bed again and tiptoed into the kitchen. She didn't want to wake anyone by turning on the lights, not that she knew where the switches were anyway, so using her phone as a flashlight again Sadie started her search at the fridge. On the top shelf was a small, covered plate with a pink post-it note that read "just in case" in neat handwriting and signed with a heart. She smiled. These just might be the most thoughtful people she had ever met.

Sadie uncovered the plate to reveal a simple sandwich and an assortment of cut veggies. It was the perfect midnight snack. She considered taking the food back to her room, but instead pulled one of the dining room chairs so that she could sit facing out the sliding glass door into the dark night. Tucking her legs underneath her, she balanced the plate on her knee. The sky was pitch black and clear, revealing a bright, full moon. Mr. Moon was staring down at her, quietly inviting her to dance in the moonlight.

"Not tonight, Mr. Moon," she answered. "My dance card is full." Sadie loved when she could get lost in her imagination. It was a world of beautiful possibility and void of the darkness that all too often threatened the peace of her real world. The last time that she had seen the moon look so brilliant was that night on the boat with Tom. She snapped a carrot hard between her teeth, angry that he had once again managed to insert himself into her thoughts.

Come on, Tom. Stay in your lane. This trip is not about you.

Sadie finished up her snack and placed her empty plate in the sink. Then, because she was feeling playful, she stood in front of the glass door and curtseyed at the moon. "Until we meet again, Mr. Moon, I bid you adieu."

Back between her cozy covers, Sadie closed her eyes and willed herself to go back to sleep. It was no use. Her body requested rest, but her mind wanted to play. She tossed and turned in vain. Staring at the ceiling, Sadie huffed in frustration. *So, this is jetlag. It's annoying.* Giving up, she turned on the lamp on the bedside table and pulled *Anne of Green Gables* out of her backpack. It had been hard to choose which books to bring with her. She opted for her favourite and hoped she would be able to find some new treasures here in the land of great literature to bring home.

Sadie spent an hour in Avonlea with Anne Shirley before her eyes began to droop. Grateful, she shut off the light and fell into a deep and luscious sleep, this time dreaming of wearing puffed sleeves and drinking raspberry cordial.

Rays of brilliant sunlight cascaded through the bedroom window. A dainty butterfly sun-catcher hung in the window greedily devouring the light, sending brilliant rainbows of colour dancing across the room. Bright beams of light fell on Sadie's eyes causing her to rouse awake. She stretched and yawned, allowing herself to meet the day.

Looking at the clock, she was shocked to see that it was already ten o'clock. It was rare for her to sleep this late at home, but back home, it was only six. Her internal clock was a mess. Sadie sat up and allowed herself a moment to once again revel in the fact that where she found herself was not in a dream. She was in England and about to spend three glorious weeks experiencing another culture, seeing world-famous sights, and walking where some of the great literary giants have walked. Her first day had been pretty much wasted on jet lag, but Sadie was feeling recharged and ready to be more socially engaged.

Plodding out of the room into the kitchen, all was quiet. There was another bright pink slip of paper on the counter. In perfectly penned cursive, it read:

> Sadie, we have gone to church. Hopefully we didn't disturb you. We have left you some breakfast on the table. Please make yourself at home. We will be back by lunch.

It was signed with another heart. Sadie presumed from the handwriting that both notes had been penned by Bridget. Placing the note back on the counter, she scoped out the kitchen and found that they had, indeed, left her breakfast—extravagant enough for the Queen herself. A place setting was elaborately laid out with fine China. A small goblet was filled with orange juice and another with milk. A large plate in the center was covered with a warmer. She lifted it to reveal baked beans, two fried eggs, bacon, slices of tomato, and toast. On a smaller plate there was a tea biscuit and a small tart. In the center of the table was a bowl full of a variety of fruit.

Sadie gaped at the elaborate display. Most days she was lucky to eat breakfast at all, and if she did, it was usually a banana or an apple. Never anything like this. Her stomach noisily declared its excitement at the feast. Sitting down to her private meal, she thought of Dylan. He would be in his glory. She laughed at the thought and then ran back to her room for her cellphone so she could snap a picture to send to Dawn.

Her best friend had given her strict instructions to document the entire trip so that she could live vicariously through Sadie. It was going to be fun to share this experience with her, although Sadie had no intentions of taking pictures of random European men, which Dawn had also requested. For that experience, Dawn was just going to have to make the trip herself.

By the time that the Burgesses returned home, Sadie had eaten, showered, and was in the middle of unpacking her bags. Hearing them enter, she met them at the door. Bridget was wearing a lovely, full-length, peach sundress. Her golden hair was pulled into a braid that trailed over one shoulder. She looked like she had just walked off the cover of a magazine. Lily looked like a doll in a poofy pink dress with a wide satin sash around her waist that tied in a bow at the back. Her hair was swept to one side with a big pink barrette, and her tiny feet were adorned with ruffled lace ankle socks and white shoes. Mark was dressed similarly to yesterday in a button-down shirt, but he had swapped the black dress pants for more casual tan slacks. They truly were a picture-perfect family. Sadie's heart ached ever so slightly at the scene that had once been very near to her own reality. She swallowed the lump in her throat and offered them a smile.

"Thank you for allowing me to sleep. I didn't realize how much the trip would take out of me. I'm feeling very rested now though."

"We completely understand. It is important to allow yourself the rest you need in the beginning so that you can be adjusted and enjoy your trip," Mark said.

"I do hope that you were able to make yourself comfortable," Bridget added.

"Oh, yes. And that breakfast was incredible, as was my midnight snack. Thank you. Surprisingly, I ate every bite, but please don't feel as though you need to serve me. I am happy to fend for myself and pitch in while I'm here." Sadie wanted to be sure that they understood she wasn't a freeloader. Although they were the ones who had brought her here, it felt wrong somehow to let them cater to her.

Bridget brushed off her concern with a wave of her hand, and Mark, who had ushered his daughter into the living room and was pulling out her toys, responded in a jovial tone. "Perfect. We have been needing someone to clean the eaves and trim the hedges. Looks like you arrived just in time." Sadie couldn't tell at first if he was joking until she saw Bridget chuck a throw pillow at his head, which he expertly ducked.

"Mark Patrick Burgess. Don't you dare torment her like that," Bridget scolded.

He laughed and shrugged. "Can't blame a man for trying." He looked at Sadie and said, "In all seriousness, you are our first houseguest, so we are just excited about it. Let us know if our enthusiasm is too much."

Sadie smiled at the good-natured banter and then asked, because she couldn't help herself, "Do you eat like that every morning?"

Mark chuckled at her comment, but it was Lily that chimed in. "I like to eat porridge for breakfast...with berries." The tot beamed with pride at the announcement as if she had made the breakfast herself.

With motherly tenderness, Bridget stroked her daughter's hair. "That's right lovey, you do. And you are growing so big because you eat all your breakfast." Bridget turned to respond to Sadie. "No, Sunday mornings Mark likes to get up early and cook us all a big feast before we head off to church. Most days we keep it simple, like porridge." Sadie smiled at Lily who was now twirling around the room to make her dress flare out. She looked like a bubblegum spinning top.

"And speaking of food," Mark said clapping in hands and rubbing them together in anticipation, "We thought we would take you out to lunch at one of our favourite places in town. It's a great little café, and it's owned by a friend of Bridget's. We can chat through some plans for your stay if you like. We are really looking forward to getting to know you better."

"That sounds lovely," Sadie answered. She blushed as she realized that she had unintentionally added a slight British accent to the word "lovely." Neither Mark nor Bridget seemed to notice, but Sadie mentally scolded herself for the imitation. It had happened before after watching the movie *Pride and Prejudice* with Dawn. She found herself slipping into a British accent for hours after it was over. *This may prove to be a challenge,* she thought.

The four of them loaded into the family vehicle, which was significantly more cramped sitting in the backseat next to Lily's car seat than the front had been. Lily, however, was pleased as punch to have Sadie's undivided attention for the drive and proceeded to tell her in detail all the things that she had done in her class at church. Apparently, the highlight of the morning was when she received a rainbow sticker for being a good listener. Her tiny voice and adorable accent melted Sadie's heart. It was hard not to immediately fall in love with the tot.

Mark pointed out their church, an old building on the corner, hemmed in by a stone fence and large oak trees. The dilapidated stone and stained glass reminded her of one of the Catholic churches that she had seen when travelling through Old Quebec.

"Methodist church? Sadie asked, slightly puzzled. I don't think I have heard of that denomination before." It didn't surprise her that the Burgesses attended church. It seemed like religion was much more embedded into the culture of this country than her own, but she was at a loss when it came to comprehending all the ins and outs of the various denominations.

"Methodist churches, a type of Protestant church, are common here, but I believe they are all over the world. We used to attend the larger one in town, and it was great, but friends invited us to this one, and we found that we preferred the smaller size. There's something great about being known and knowing everyone," Mark explained.

"That's a matter of opinion," Sadie mumbled under her breath. Her thoughts travelled to Lunenburg and the suffocating closeness of everyone knowing her business. Loud enough for everyone to hear she responded, "Oh, I suppose that can be nice sometimes." In her heart, Sadie felt that being truly known and seen was a much more stressful way to live. Blending in with the crowd seemed like the perfect solution to her problems. Once again Sadie felt walls going up around her heart. Getting to know Mark and his family was one thing but being vulnerable with them would be another thing entirely.

Chapter Twelve

Downtown Chipping Norton looked nothing like Lunenburg. Back home could be characterized by three things: colour, space, and water. This town was compact, quaint, and shockingly void of any variation of colour. Everything was beige. Or brown. Or beige and brown. With the exception of the green provided by the foliage, every street was crowded with row upon row of sandy-toned stonework.

Mark expertly parallel parked their car in an open space along the side of a street with various shops and eateries, all of which looked incredibly enticing to Sadie. She was excited for her first outing in a new country and was very ready to experience authentic English cuisine—even with the breakfast feast she had just consumed a couple hours earlier.

Sadie carefully extricated herself from the compact space and followed closely as they walked down the narrow sidewalk. Mark led the way, carrying Lily, and Bridget explained that the café they were going to was a favourite of theirs. Elora's, as it was called, was owned by a lady from their church and offered some of the best coffee and danishes in town, according to Mark.

They stopped in front of an unassuming door next to a tiny window, above which was a hand painted wooden sign that read "Elora's Café & Bistro." An earthy looking woman met the group of four at the door of the café. She had wild, red curls pulled up into a clip and clunky bangles on her arms. Loose pants were topped with a moss green blouse over which she wore a long macrame vest. She was striking and about her was an air of humble confidence—poised, yet open and welcoming. The woman embraced Bridget and kissed her on the cheek.

"Bridget, darling, it is wonderful to see you. Would you like your usual table?"

"Please. With an extra chair for our guest." Bridget gestured to the woman. "Sadie, I'd like you to meet my dear friend, Pia."

With Bridget's accent, Sadie was certain she had heard Bridget call the woman, Pier. The name was unfamiliar, but Sadie assumed that it was a cultural difference like calling the trunk of a car the boot. She smiled warmly and said as politely as she could, "It's nice to meet you, Pier. What a lovely café you have."

Mark, Bridget, and Pia exchanged subtle smiles at the error. "Her name is actually Pia," Mark explained. "P-I-A. The Brits tend to add an -er sound to the end of words ending in 'a.'".

Sadie was mortified. "Oh, I'm so sorry."

"Not to worry. Easy mistake. I certainly made several of those when I first moved here. You'll get the hang of it," Mark said.

"Exactly. Think nothing of it," Pia said graciously extending her hand to Sadie. "Sadie, welcome to Elora's. I have heard so much about you. What a gift that finding you has been for Mark and his family." As other customers entered behind them, Pia excused herself and left them in the care of a waitress who ushered them to their seats.

The inside of the café was a hidden treasure, a stark contrast to its unassuming exterior. Large, exposed, dark wooden beams lined the ceiling, between which soft lights were hung low over what appeared to be handmade tables. Large slabs of tree trunk had been worked into unique tables, each its own piece of art. They were hugged by thin chairs padded in a rich purple fabric. Soft jazz music added to the ambience of the room. The atmosphere was warm and inviting, but Sadie's favourite part of the café was the large shelving unit behind front counter lined with dozens and dozens of hot drink cups. There were coffee mugs, teacups, espresso cups—all shapes and sizes and colours—each one unique. The display took up most of the wall and was a stunning piece of artistry.

Sadie paused as they walked past.

"Impressive, isn't it?" Mark asked.

"It's beautiful. I love that they are all different," Sadie answered.

"It's practical, too," he added. "Each guest who orders a hot drink gets to choose the cup they like best to drink from—that was Pia's idea. She realized that one of the things she enjoyed when visiting her friends for tea was choosing her own cup. She wanted this café to feel as though you were a 'welcomed friend.'" He pointed to a hand painted sign on the wall that read "Welcome Friends." Sadie thought it was a lovely, personal touch and one that made her immediately fonder of the woman with the wild, red curls.

Once seated at their table, Sadie perused the menu offered to her. Everything sounded so delicious that it was hard to decide. These kinds of decisions had always been panic-inducing for Sadie, who wanted to make the exact right choice. In the end, she typically resorted to tried and true dishes. Today was no different. She opted for a simple soup and sandwich combo, which was probably the right choice considering how much she had already eaten that day. She did, however, enthusiastically agree when Mark insisted that they also order tea and scones with clotted cream and jam. Sadie was excited to experience all that England had to offer, and tea and scones was on the top of her list, right after fish and chips. After spending three summers slinging fish and fries, she was curious to see how the original compared to the East Coast copycat.

"Well, Sadie," Mark began, interrupting her thoughts, "if it's okay with you we would like to pray and give thanks for our food and for you."

Sadie nodded. As she had done with Lynn and Jack for years, and even with Tom until recently, she would politely and respectfully participate in their faith practices, so long as they did not require any commitment on her part. As Mark bowed his head, the rest of them did the same.

"Father God, we give you thanks today for your faithfulness and love. Thank you for Sadie and for bringing us together. We ask that you would bless her, and that this visit be a time of joy and connection for us all. Fill her with your peace. Thank you for Pia and a place for us to gather around a table as friends. Thank you for good food and family with which to enjoy it. In Jesus' name we pray. Amen."

Sadie found herself touched at his prayer. Peace was something of a foreign concept for her. Since the accident and her parents' passing, Sadie had found ways to cope and to find joy, but a deep peace at the cards she had been dealt was something that was simply out of reach. She found that excelling in school had offered her a distraction and reading had offered her an escape. Between the two, she was able to keep any unsettled feelings at bay, though lately it was becoming more difficult. Tom's entrance into her world, and now Mark's, had thrown off any semblance of control she felt she had on her life and emotions.

"Thank you for that," Sadie said. "It was very kind."

"Any time. So," he rubbed his hands together as in anticipation, "we had some ideas about sightseeing while you were here, but we would love to know what you had hoped to see. London, of course, and all the major attractions—London Bridge, Big Ben, Westminster Abbey, Buckingham Palace. We thought we would make a weekend trip out of it so you can see it all. If you are comfortable with that. Lily's grandparents have already agreed to take her for a couple of nights so that we can have a little more flexibility."

"That would be incredible," Sadie gushed. It was thrilling to think about being able to touch and feel and smell the places she had only visited before in her daydreams. There was so much she wanted to see; the past twenty-four hours had only whetted her appetite to experience all that this beautiful country had to offer.

"Honestly, I will be so grateful for anything that I am able to see. This place is beautiful and has so much history. It's quite a bit different from back home. The oldest buildings we have are probably a hundred years old."

Bridget nodded in agreement. "It's true. History is rich everywhere in this country. The tourist sights are a spectacular tribute to that and certainly a must to visit, but there is also a richness to learning and appreciating the culture authentically. Like here at Elora's, for instance. You will learn more about the Brits and our culture in these settings than anywhere else." She gave Sadie a wink and said, "See all you can, but just make sure that you go home with more than just a double-decker bus keychain. Make some memories that will last."

"'The traveler sees what he sees. The tourist sees what he has come to see.' G.K. Chesteron." Mark spoke the words with a passionate fire. When Sadie gave him a puzzled look, he added, "Chesterton is one of my favourite British writers. He was a predecessor to writers like Lewis and Tolkien. Ever heard of him?"

Sadie shook her head. She had not.

"He's one of the greats, in my opinion. That quote just means that tourists come to a place with their eyes fixed on specific sights and because of that they risk seeing and experiencing the fullness of a place. Be a traveler. Just see what you see."

It was all excellent advice. Sadie did not want to just be a tourist. She wanted to appreciate this new place authentically. Looking around the room, she knew that these were the kinds of hidden treasures that she wanted to experience more than anything. Well, almost anything.

She chewed her lip nervously before responding. "I really hope that I can do that well. But…there is one place that I would really love to be able to visit."

"What's that?" Mark asked.

"I know that it's kind of a long shot, but I would love to visit Oxford and, if it isn't a crazy suggestion, to see the Bodelian library."

Mark sat back in his seat and smiled.

Lily looked up from the colouring page she was intent on, finally engaging in the grown ups' conversation. "I like the library. I get to do crafts there," she said, once again her R sounding very much like a W.

Bridget handed Lily a cracker out of her purse and stroked her hair affectionately. "Not that library, Lovey. The big one in Oxford."

"You have impeccable taste," Mark said. "Not all tourists even know what that is. I don't think that you will be able to go deep inside without a library card, but we can definitely plan for a day or two in Oxford. It's close enough to here. The Bodelian is worth seeing, even if it's just a guided tour. There are lots of other great adventures to be had in that city, too."

The thought of going to Oxford thrilled Sadie all the way to her toes. Since her earliest memories of reading about Lewis' Narnia, Sadie had been drawn to the land of literature—Oxford—specifically since it had been C. S. Lewis' home. Only in the last year or so as she began researching post-secondary schools had she learned about the library and the fact that it was one of the largest in the country. It was a book-lover's dream.

Their food had arrived, and so the conversation lulled as they savoured their meals. Sadie chose a delicate dusty rose teacup in which to take her tea. It was trimmed in gold, and the whole of the inside was painted with roses. There was something intriguing about the artwork being on the inside, as though it were a secret gift to the drinker. Holding the fragile cup, she felt elegant and poised.

Pia stopped at their table to inquire about how they were doing.

It was easy for Sadie to be complimentary. "Everything is delicious, and your café is really beautiful. I absolutely love the wall of cups—it's so...artistic."

"Ah, yes. The wall has become a popular feature of our establishment. I do love it when art and practicality meet, but I especially love when that art can be seen as a metaphor for life. We are all different, you know. We all serve different purposes, but together," she enmeshed her fingers to further illustrate her point, "we are beautiful." She paused and glanced back at the wall. Sadie did the same, allowing the truth to settle on her. "And I love how each customer's choice speaks a little about their personality. It allows patrons to feel at home here."

Pia placed a hand on Mark's shoulder and then gave Bridget a peck on the cheek. She thanked them for coming before continuing in her rounds about the restaurant.

Sadie did feel at home. Pia's intentionality in her design had hit its mark. Sadie wondered what her cup choice said about her.

Lily was beginning to get fussy, which Bridget said was an indication it was time to get back for her nap. They packed up and headed home, but not before Sadie snapped a couple pictures of her teacup and the artistic wall. She wanted to always remember this place and how it made her feel.

Back at their home, Bridget took Lily to rest while Mark poured he and Sadie hot cocoa and suggested they sit and chat. The afternoon sun was flooding through the windows and spilling its warm light across the room. Sadie chose to sit in the armchair directly in the sun, allowing the light's warm embrace to calm her nervous spirit. This was why she had come. This was the conversation that had caused turbulent waves in the pit of her stomach since graduation night.

Mark took a sip of his hot cocoa. "I know that we seem to be saying this a lot, but it means a lot that you would put your life on hold and come all this way for a stranger."

"You aren't a stranger, exactly. And I am grateful, too. Thank you for flying me here and hosting me. It has always been a dream of mine to travel like this." Sadie took a sip of her hot cocoa, too, and was pleasantly surprised at how rich and chocolatey it was. This was not the hot chocolate that she was used to from back home. "Wow, this is good!"

Mark chuckled and nodded. "It's Cadbury, a very popular brand of cocoa here. It's made with hot milk, which I think is the secret."

Sadie took another sip, letting the rich, sweet liquid linger on her tongue. "My uncle calls me his choc-o-holic. It may be my weakness."

"Tell me more about your aunt and uncle. What are they like?"

"They are two of the kindest and most generous people that I know. Classic small-town people. Jack would do anything to help someone, and Aunt Lynn is so hospitable. She can't help but try to feed people. I would be 300 pounds if she had her way. They have certainly always loved me as their own."

"So it's been good for you then, to be in their care all these years?" Mark seemed genuinely interested.

Sadie considered how much to share with Mark, but she decided that as his closest living family, she owed it to him to be as honest as possible. "Yes. It has been great to be raised by family, especially family who could love me so well. But..." She paused, choosing her words carefully, wanting to be truthful and yet also wanting to show respect for the two people who had devoted their lives to her care.

"It hasn't always been an easy road. We all had to navigate the grief of losing Mom and Dad. It made the early years together rocky. There were a lot of arguments in the beginning. Life at home got better as we found strategies to manage our grief, but Lynn and Jack have always struggled a little with knowing how firmly to parent. They have never wanted to force themselves into the role of being my parents, but as a result they have been pretty lax when it comes to rules or boundaries. I know that sounds like it would be a kid's dream. The problem was that I felt myself floundering a lot, just hoping that someone would give me a straight yes or no answer and not a 'we trust you to do what's best' type of response. I guess it made me feel like I was still having to parent myself a lot with the tough stuff, ya know."

"It sounds to me like you have carried some heavy burdens over the years. That is a lot of responsibility," Mark said, thoughtfully.

Sadie shrugged, but inwardly she was mentally recounting the times where she had set her own personal boundaries. Curfews, dating, dress codes. Lynn and Jack's approach had always been more suggestion than rules, trusting her to do the right thing. Thankfully for them, Sadie's internal moral compass was strong, and her desire to make minimal waves was even stronger.

Mark set his mug on the end table beside the sofa and leaned forward, his arms resting on his knees. "I know that this," he gestured back and forth between the two of them, "probably still feels pretty strange. Out of the blue you are forced to share your mother with a stranger. I also understand that it might be hard to talk about her, but, whenever you feel ready, I would really love to know anything and everything about your mom. My mom."

Sadie stared into her mug as though she could pull strength from it. The truth was that remembering her mother was a good thing, a helpful thing. Early on, the memory of her parents was like a knife in her heart. She thought about them all the time and sobbed into her pillow each night. It was agony. In every sense, she had felt lost and empty. A part of her had desperately wanted to forget so that she could be free of the pain. Her counsellor said that it was important to preserve the memory of her parents by allowing herself to remember them as they had been and to treasure the good times. It was a difficult practice without letting despair and self-pity overwhelm her, but a more frightening fear lingered in the corners of her heart—a fear that she would forget them altogether. There were days that Sadie had woken in panic, drenched in sweat, because she was unable to pull a clear picture of their face to the forefront of her mind. Those days she struggled to remember the way her mom's hair smelled as Sadie buried her head in her shoulder or the way her daddy's hands felt around her waist as he would toss her into the air.

No, it wasn't easy. In fact, in many ways, Sadie was still reeling from the shock that she had experienced over her mother's secret past. But she owed it to Mark to be a window into the life of the mother he never would know. She was, after all, his closest connection to her. Selfishly, she knew that the more she shared the memories the more cemented they would become in her mind. That fact alone spurred her on, and from that realization, she drew the courage to share with Mark.

"You look a lot like her." Sadie said. "You share her smile and you have the same eyes, too." Mark smiled and leaned back into the cushions, silently urging Sadie to continue.

"My mom," she paused and corrected herself, "our mom was amazing. She was so compassionate and gentle. I remember this one time that we were running errands downtown, and there was a homeless man asleep on the bench by the docks. He wasn't even asking for anything, but Mom went and bought him some food and a blanket and left it for him on the bench. That was Mom. She was always looking for ways to help people without asking for any thanks in return."

"That's so good," Mark encouraged. "Keep going."

"And we would have the silliest dance parties in the kitchen while she made supper. Family was really important to her," Sadie stopped abruptly, the weight of her words landed like rocks in her stomach. Pain flashed across Mark's eyes before he looked away and composed himself. "I'm so sorry. I didn't mean…"

"No, no. It's okay. I want you to be able to speak freely." He rubbed a hand over his chin and looked thoughtfully out the window beyond Sadie. "You know, before you continue, I wonder if maybe it would be helpful for you to know a little about my story." Sadie nodded for him to continue. "I could not have asked for better parents—my adopted ones, I mean. Rob and Margaret Burgess. They had tried to have children of their own for years, but after a lot of heartbreak they gave up trying and made the decision to adopt."

"I was theirs from the time I was only a few hours old. They gave me the world—nice house, clothes, trips, toys. They were at every one of my hockey games. Mom would bundle up with extra blankets because the rinks were so cold. Even if it was a six a.m. practice, she would be there. They were two of the best parents anyone could ask for."

"Were?" Sadie asked tentatively.

"My dad died when I was sixteen in a freak construction accident. My mom passed away just over a year ago after a three-year battle with breast cancer. It was shortly after that when I decided to hire Detective Adams and to start looking for my birth family. I didn't want to cause my mom any more pain, so I couldn't bring myself to search for you while she was alive.

"It was hard losing Dad as a teen. I know quite a bit about the darkness of grief. I lashed out in anger a lot in the beginning. Mom was a saint. She patiently took it while carrying her own pain. Those years are key to figuring out who you are, so it was a significant blow. I'm grateful that my parents had always taken me to church with them. They instilled in me a strong faith—one that helped me to weather the storm of grief and make it out of that season intact."

Sadie understood his pain, and she was grateful that, in a small way, he could understand hers. Despite her own reservations about God, she envied the faith that Mark spoke of, and the peace that he seemed to have in speaking of his parents' passing.

"I'm so sorry for your loss. Did your mom live here in England?"

"No, she stayed in Sudbury, Ontario, in our family home after dad died. When she got sick, we hired caretakers to be with her around the clock, and I made sure to visit as often as I could. In the end, all three of us travelled back home for two months. I wanted to be there with her at the end. It wasn't easy, but looking back now, I know that it was the right decision."

"I'm sure it meant the world to her for you all to be there." Sadie then had a realization. Mark must have been heartbroken when he learned about her mom and dad's accident. Had he looked for them when he was of age, maybe he could have met his birth mother. She broached the topic tentatively. "Were you...were you very upset to learn about Mom and the accident?"

"I had a few hard days, sure. I had come so far only to have the door shut in my face. I would never get to know the woman who birthed me. Never get to look her in the eyes or hear her voice or to know what parts of me were from her. It was a different kind of grief. But it wasn't completely hopeless. I had found you, and I felt in my spirit that you would be someone I would need in my life."

Mark paused his story to take another sip of his cocoa before refocusing his attention on Sadie. He spoke deliberately and earnestly. "Sadie, when my mom died, I felt untethered. Like I was adrift in this world. Yes, I had Bridget and Lily, but my own family, my flesh and blood were all gone. Finding my birth family, finding you, has filled that void."

"I'm glad that we found each other, too." Sadie didn't know what else to say. The intensity made her feel awkward. Mark seemed to sense that because he shifted gears.

"I know that this isn't the easiest conversation to have. We can pick it up again another time. Want to help me prep for dinner? I thought we could make homemade Yorkshire puddings to go with our roast."

Sadie felt relief in the reprieve from the heaviness. It was good, though, to open up to Mark. In many ways, he was the only other person who could truly understand what it meant to lose her parents. That thought was surprisingly comforting.

Following Mark into the kitchen, Sadie couldn't help but wonder just what other surprises the rest of her trip might have for her.

Chapter Thirteen

Friday morning dawned slowly as the sun struggled to make itself seen from behind the fluffy clouds. In spite of the dreary morning, Sadie couldn't sleep. She welcomed the morning with more excitement than a child on Christmas morning, and although it was still quite early, threw off the covers and leapt out of bed. One could simply not lie in bed when a world that had only existed in your mind's eye was about to become a reality. Oxford beckoned to her, and she was more than ready to answer the call.

She had been in Chipping Norton with Mark and Bridget for almost a week, and while the town was lovely, she was ready to broaden her British horizons. The Burgesses were very gracious hosts and were quickly becoming good friends. She was enjoying herself, with the exception of a few awkward moments.

Sadie cringed as she recalled the time during their supper meal when Lily had asked her if she had a boyfriend. The question had taken her by surprise. Judging from the way Mark choked on his bite of curry, it was safe to say he was surprised too. Were three-year-olds supposed to know about boyfriends? Sadie had chewed her bite very slowly to give herself time to process a suitable answer for the doting girl.

"I do have friends that are boys. Is that what you mean?" Sadie asked, tentatively.

Lily cocked her head and tapped a tiny pointer finger along the side of her jaw. "No. I mean like daddy is mommy's boyfriend. They kiss and hug and stuff."

Sadie could feel her cheeks flushing as all eyes turned to her. She opted to keep her answer simple. "No, I don't have one." Graciously, Lily seemed content with her response and turned her attention back to her food as though nothing had happened. Bridget had quietly chided her daughter about asking things that are personal or private to a guest.

Outwardly, Sadie had played it off as a darling little bit of humour, but internally, it had taken several moments for Sadie to regain her equilibrium. She had been doing considerably well at keeping thoughts of Tom at bay. Now a three-year-old who knew next to nothing of romantic relationships was able cause her brain to conjure up thoughts of him once again. She wished that things had ended differently between them. It would be nice to be able to share some of her adventure with him. Sadie knew that he would be interested in hearing about it, and she knew that he would approve of her building a relationship with Mark and his family.

She shook off the recollection. All of that was behind her because today would be a momentous day for Sadie Elizabeth Jones. Today she would walk the same cobblestone streets that some of the greatest literary giants had walked. She would gaze up in wonder at the Dreaming Spires—a term coined in poetry to describe the iconic architecture of

Oxford. She would breathe the dust of books hundreds of years old. Sadie was giddy with excitement. She made sure to dress comfortably for a day of walking and to pack her phone and journal to document the day. There was something about being here that made her want to connect more with pen and paper than she had in a long time.

Slinging her purse across her body, she did a double take in the full-length mirror attached to the back of the guest room door. Her auburn curls hung low, still damp from her early morning shower. A flowered scrunchie adorned her wrist if the inevitable need occurred for her to tame the tresses. She wore light wash jeans with comfortable sneakers (it still felt strange to have shoes on inside). A simple, navy V-neck tee shirt that she had tucked into her jeans completed the ensemble; the locket that Lynn and Jack had given her glimmered around her neck. Sadie assessed the person staring back at her and gave her a contented nod. The last month had matured her. She no longer felt like a silly high school girl, but like a sophisticated young woman who could navigate relationships, manage unexpected circumstances, and jet set to new countries.

And now that young woman was about to have a new adventure.

Culture, history, art—it was all there, waiting for her to dive in. The world was a big place. She couldn't wait to prove to her friends and family, and, if she were honest, to herself, that she was destined for more than small-town life where you are never able to become any other version of yourself than the one the local townspeople write for you. That world had too long shackled her to the trauma of her past. The world before her was one of opportunity, growth, and adventure. She was more than ready.

Bridget had arranged for Lily to spend the day with her grandparents, which would allow the trio to experience the city more freely, unencumbered by the needs of a young child. Mark had just returned from dropping her off as Sadie and Bridget were finishing a quick scone and tea for breakfast. Sadie had never been much of a tea drinker, but she was certainly getting used to having an English breakfast tea with a little milk in the mornings. It made her feel cultured.

"Do we have everything we need? Everyone have their wallets? Anyone need to go to the loo before we head out?" Mark asked, clearly taking his role as tour guide very seriously.

"I think we are ready, Dear," Bridget replied.

With significant gusto, Sadie added, "I have never been more ready for anything in my life." She paused, looking back and forth between Mark and Bridget, both of whom were holding back a smile. Sadie grimaced. "Too much? Sorry, I'm just excited. I promise to dial it back a notch so we don't stick out like tacky tourists."

"Nonsense," Bridget said, brushing the self-deprecation away with a graceful wave of her hand. Sadie would never tell her this for fear of offending her, but Bridget reminded her of a Disney princess in the way she carried herself. "Your enthusiasm is delightful, and we shall make every effort to embrace our role as tourists. Today is a day to do all the touristy things. Mark and I are looking forward to seeing the city through fresh eyes, especially ones so passionate about it all."

"That's very kind of you," Sadie responded.

"Alright, enough chatting. Time to head out, or we'll miss our train." Mark ushered them out the door into the sunshine. The train station was a short walk from their home, so it made more sense to head there by foot than to take the car. Mark said that in England it was more common to travel by train, bike, or foot than by car because of the limited parking and congested roads. Sadie was grateful to have a practical place to put her energy as they traipsed through the town.

The train station was small, quaint, and much more outdated in its technology than Sadie would have expected. They purchased their tickets from a man at the wicket and waited outside on a long, hard, bench along the back of the station. Sadie sat for a moment, but couldn't contain her energy, so she opted for pacing along the platform. The train arrived promptly at nine o'clock, and the threesome filed in, walking to the back of the car, where there were several vacant seats. Sadie grabbed one near the window and peered out of the glass.

As they rolled forward, the intercoms boomed with the monotone voice of a train conductor listing off the upcoming stops, most of which Sadie could barely decipher given the thick accent and unfamiliar names. Mark and Bridget chatted in quiet tones across from her about the plans for the day; Sadie felt free to allow her mind to wander through the dreamy countryside that danced past her window. It was picturesque and sprawling and everything that she imagined it would be. She could almost picture a nineteenth century shepherdess reclining in the fields under the shade of an alder tree.

This was what she wanted. This was what she had been chasing. Life outside the walls of Lunenburg. It may have been offered to her in a surprising and unconventional way, but nonetheless, it was everything she hoped it would be.

After about twenty minutes and several short stops, they exited the train station and Sadie took a deep, satisfied breath, on which she promptly choked. The air was not as fresh as the rolling sheep-filled meadows would have led her to believe. She took a second breath, slower this time, doing her best to decipher the malodorous scents. From what she could tell, car exhaust and cigarette fumes mingled to create an odour that burned her nostrils.

Mark read the look on her face and smiled. "You get used to it. Come on, we are headed this way." He took off ahead of the two ladies, walking at a brisk pace. Sadie loved that he was so invested in his role as tour guide, but she was not sure if her legs could keep up with his pace. Thankfully, Bridget linked arms with her and matched her gait.

"Never mind Mark. He takes these kinds of activities very seriously. He will realize we aren't right behind him soon enough." She giggled mischievously and Sadie couldn't help but feel at ease with Bridget by her side.

They passed a huge parking lot filled with more bicycles than Sadie had ever seen at one time. There must have been hundreds. She stopped and gaped at the scene, pulling out her phone to take a picture. "Whoa! That's crazy!" She exclaimed loudly, stepping closer to frame the shot. "Dawn will never believe this." Without watching where she was going, Sadie stepped into the bike lane and was nearly sideswiped by a cyclist who skillfully dodged the pedestrian in his path.

A couple of men in business attire who were walking past scoffed loudly. "Ignorant Americans," one grunted at them.

Sadie's cheeks flushed. "I'm Canadian," she responded meekly, but they were gone.

Bridget grimaced, ever so slightly, at the exchange. Mark, who had finally realized their lackadaisical stroll had not kept up with his stride, had doubled back in time to witness the faux pas and offer some gentle advice.

"Perhaps it might be more helpful if you saw this country's differences as an opportunity to see the world from a different perspective rather than as odd or peculiar. Oh, and always be sure to avoid stopping or standing in the bike lane."

"I'm sorry about that. I didn't mean to be rude; I just thought it was really cool." Sadie's shoulders slumped, the embarrassment deflating her mood. But Bridget was quick to offer grace and encouragement.

"Don't worry a tap about that, lovey. They were the rude ones. You needn't concern yourself with it anymore."

"Thanks Bridget."

Mark was openly impatient now. "Okay you two. I was trying to keep it a secret, but we really need to get moving. Ben's Cookies is opening in a few minutes, and we have to be there in time to get them fresh and hot."

"Ben's Cookies?" Sadie questioned.

"Only the best cookie you will ever eat in your life," Mark stated plainly as he resumed his brisk pace ahead of them. Sadie didn't question, but this time she hastened her pace and followed closely behind. Cookies were a sufficient motivator for her any day, but especially with a claim like that.

Mark's pursuit did not disappoint. Tucked away in the covered market was a tiny, unassuming, red kiosk with black, scratchy lettering across the front and a mouth-watering display of cookies piled in the front jewel case. All of the cookies were loaded with massive chunks of chocolate or other specialty ingredients, and they were so thick that you paid by the weight, not the quantity. Sadie opted to try a classic milk chocolate chunk, while Bridget chose white chocolate and cranberry and Mark, milk chocolate and peanut butter. He bought a fourth double chocolate chunk and added it to Sadie's bag.

"For later," he winked. "But make sure to save room for lunch. We are taking you somewhere really special."

They all stepped to a quiet corner of the market away from the foot traffic to devour their delicious morsels. Sadie let the first bite linger in her mouth. *Wow. This is incredible,* she thought. She would have said it aloud, but she was too busy savouring the mouthful. It was the most decadent cookie she remembered ever eating. It was crispy on the outside, but dense and chewy and chocolatey on the inside. And it was still warm. Mark was right to hurry them along for this. She was especially grateful for the extra one now tucked in her purse, though quite certain they would need to come back here again so she could stock up. *I wonder if these would stay fresh long enough for me to bring them home. Who am I kidding? They would never make it that far before I ate them.*

They all sighed contentedly as the last crumbs were devoured. Sadie took a moment to wipe any lingering evidence from her mouth, and then she had Mark snap a picture of her standing in front of the little kiosk. She quickly posted it to her social media with the hashtag "best cookie ever" before they set off again, this time in the direction of the Bodelian library. As they walked, Sadie was a little surprised to see that so much of the town was quite urban. Recognizable shops and restaurants lined the streets, punctuated by the occasional stone building. Given the city's rich history, she had expected it to feel more like she was entering the past and less as though she were navigating a booming metropolis.

They had come to the end of the street, and as they turned the corner, Sadie gaped at the sight. This was so much more like what she had imagined the "City of Spires" to be like. Urban storefronts gave way to lofty stone buildings weathered by time. The streets felt smaller as high walls closed in tightly to the concrete road. The beautiful stonework architecture flaunted the city's tradition of prestige, academia, and status.

She recognized the Bodleian library right away from the research she had done prior to her trip. The circular building with its pillars, dome roof, and spire were too unique to miss. Bridget pointed out that what Sadie was recognizing was, in fact, the Radcliffe Camera, or the Rad Cam, one of the library's more iconic buildings. The Bodleian, in fact, spans over several blocks and multiple buildings. Bridget didn't want to give away too much information so as not to ruin the tour, but she informed Sadie that it is one of the oldest libraries in Europe and it houses more than thirteen million printed items. The enormity of it was hard for her to fathom. Given that, at least in Sadie's mind, Europe is the birthplace of great literature, this felt like a momentous moment.

"Where do they house all those books?" Sadie questioned.

Bridget smiled and pulled her hand across her lips as though zipping them. "I've said too much already. That's what the tour is for."

Sadie pulled out her phone to post a picture of the Radcliffe Camera to her social and saw that the picture of her in front of Ben's Cookies already had over fifty likes. She also noticed that there was a text message from Tom. Her thumb hovered over the button for a moment before she decided to open it. It was only a funny gif about England. Under normal circumstances it probably would have made her chuckle. *Geez, this guy is not making it easy on me.* Every time she was certain that he was out of her life and out of her mind, he would pop up somewhere.

She was about to turn off her phone in an attempt to shut out any thought of Tom when it started buzzing. The screen ID told her that Aunt Lynn was trying to video chat. There were still ten minutes before their tour, so Sadie accepted the call, holding the phone up so that the buildings behind her were visible in the camera.

"Hi Auntie!"

"Well, hello! It looks like you made it to Oxford." Sadie giggled as her aunt and uncle attempted to squeeze together so that they could both be seen in the frame. Lynn and Jack had been faithfully checking in with her via daily texts and the occasional quick phone call, but for the most part, they had graciously shown trust in Sadie by giving her some much needed space during this adventure. They didn't pry or demand updates. Sadie was thankful for both the check-ins and the space.

"We did! And we are about to take a tour of the Bodleian Library. It's the largest in Europe. Oh and, Jack—Mark took us to get cookies at the most amazing little spot. You would love them."

Jack smiled. "You know me well, girlie. Sounds like you guys are having a dandy time."

"Definitely. I can't wait to tell you all about it and show you all my pictures." She panned the camera around so that they could see the area as she was seeing it.

"It looks incredible," replied Lynn. "You know that we will be excited to hear all your stories. But for now, you had better get back to living them."

"And maybe see if that cookie place will deliver across the pond, will ya?" Jack asked jokingly. Sadie just rolled her eyes.

"Make sure that you're drinking lots of water if you're doing a lot of walking," Lynn chimed in.

Typical Lynn. Sadie pulled a water bottle from her purse and held it up as proof, fighting the urge to roll her eyes at that comment as well. "Don't worry, I am. Mark and Bridget are taking wonderful care of me."

"That's so good to hear. Now, go have fun. We just wanted to check in."

Sadie appreciated the gesture. She blew them a kiss into the camera. "Love you both."

"We love you, too," they both responded before hanging up the call.

There were still a couple minutes before their tour was to begin so Sadie used her phone to snap a few more pictures, including some selfies with Mark and Bridget. Promptly at eleven, they met their tour in front of the Rad Cam, as Bridget called it. A tall, gangly young man with large glasses perched on his nose and wearing a well-fitted suit jacket introduced himself as their tour guide, Colin. He was a student at Magdalen College studying economics, but he worked at the Bod part-time. Sadie tried not to fixate on the fact that he had to push his glasses up off his nose every few minutes or that he talked excessively with his hands as he spoke. Instead, as they walked, she listened to the history of the building as she drank in the sights, wishing she was allowed to take pictures or explore on her own.

According to Colin, the library is over 400 years old and is the second largest in Britain with the majority of its books being housed underground. With over forty libraries and reading rooms across several buildings in Oxford, access to materials works very differently than most libraries. Being a reference library, materials are never actually checked out or borrowed. Instead, an intricate system of ordering books or materials from the underground is in place to allow readers an opportunity to access the materials inside the buildings.

"Now if you have never had a membership to the library or tried to become a reader here, this may come as a surprise to you. Every person wishing to obtain access to the library must swear an oath. This was originally an oral declaration, but now it is usually accomplished by signing a letter. However, if you are an external reader then you will still be required to recite the declaration orally before receiving admittance. Does anyone know what the oath states?"

The group was quiet. Sadie looked at Bridget who merely grinned and gave her a subtle wink.

There was no response, so the guide pulled a card from his pocket and read. "It states:

> I hereby undertake not to remove from the Library, nor to mark, deface, or injure in any way, any volume, document or other object belonging to it or in its custody; not to bring into the Library, or kindle therein, any fire or flame, and not to smoke in the Library; and I promise to obey all rules of the Library." He looked at the group and smiled.

"So, if anyone had plans to kindle fire, you're going to have to do that somewhere else."

Sadie and a couple others politely chuckled at his lame joke. It was fascinating to see how little had changed over the years or perhaps how intentionally tradition was embedded into the modern life of the library.

As they walked, Colin talked about other points of interest to the group. The library—named after Sir Thomas Bodley—housed a Gutenberg bible, one of only twenty-one remaining, and Shakespeare's first folio from 1623. It has also been the location for several famous movie scenes, including *Harry Potter*. Colin noted significant connections to monarchs, prime ministers, nobles, scholars, and authors while pointing out the iconic Gothic architecture. All of that was impressive, but none of it made Sadie's jaw drop as much as walking through the grandiose reading rooms with their vaulted ceilings and shelves that stretched from floor to ceiling laden with books. Ladders were positioned against the shelves to reach the first level of books, and a short balcony stretched around the room providing access to the upper shelves. It was breathtaking. Sadie longed to be left alone in the room to explore the titles and get lost in the pages.

After about an hour of touring the buildings, Colin ended the tour at a gift shop inside the Radcliffe Camera. Sadie chose to purchase a few postcards showcasing the inside of the library since she hadn't been allowed to take pictures. Exiting the building, she squinted as her eyes adjusted to the light. The sun had managed to chase away the clouds and was now startlingly bright for those who had been walking through dark corridors and dimly lit rooms. Sadie pulled her sunglasses out of her purse, grateful she remembered to bring them with her at the last minute.

"We are really close to where I went to college," Bridget said. "Would you like to stop in and see it?"

"It really is worth a visit," Mark added.

Sadie knew that Bridget had gone to school here at Regent's Park College, but she had not wanted to overstep in asking for a personal tour. It seemed like Oxford Colleges were too elite or prestigious for drop in visitors. "I would love that, if you are sure it's okay." Sadie responded.

"Of course. We won't be able to tour it all, but it shouldn't be an issue to at least pop in and see the quad. It's on the way."

Sadie wasn't sure where it was on the way to, but she did not bother questioning. It wasn't a far walk before Bridget stopped in front of a small door in the wall. It seemed out of place with no signage or alcove. Just a solitary door in a long, high stone wall. Bridget opened it and stepped in.

The white tile floor, plain white walls, and dated window treatments were unpretentious and slightly underwhelming. Sadie was a little surprised at the building's interior given that her experience thus far with Oxford had been ornate and extravagant. Bridget seemed to read her expression because she offered an explanation.

"Regent's Park is one of the smaller colleges. I have always appreciated that about it. It feels homier and more accessible than some of the larger ones. Come on, I want to show you the quad."

They walked through the hallway to an open, grassy rectangle hemmed in on all four sides by the building. The large trees in the center and the foliage that enveloped one of the brick walls were in full bloom. It was an explosion of colour. Stunning. Standing here Sadie had a better understanding of the size of the college than she got from the door in the wall. Beautiful brick walls with oversized latticed windows stretched the length of a city block. Several students lounged across the warm grass or sat on benches reading. This felt collegiate. This was how Sadie imagined university life to be. It made her both excited and nervous for her own academic adventure to Dalhousie in the fall.

"This is so lovely, Bridget. If I were a student here, I would never want to leave the quad."

"It is beautiful, but much more enjoyable at this time of year than in the winter. The cozy corners of the library are a more appealing study locale when it's cold."

Mark cleared his throat. "Okay, ladies, this has been fun, but I'm starving. The cookie is long gone. Ready to head to lunch?" He rubbed his stomach as further proof of his hunger.

Bridget and Sadie heartily agreed. They were both hungry too, and after so much walking, a nice sit-down meal would be great.

Leaving the school, Sadie thanked Bridget for the detour. It meant a lot to see even a small picture of what university life was like in this part of the world. As they turned the corner onto St. Giles Street, Sadie let out a squeal of delight. She had hoped but had dared not openly wish for this stop in case she were wrong. In front of her was The Eagle and Child, the meeting place of the Inklings, a group of writers that included C.S. Lewis and J.R.R. Tolkein. It was the most unassuming building tucked neatly between an alleyway and a modern convenience store. Sadie had read the entire *Chronicles of Narnia* series when she was ten and then spent an entire month learning everything she could about Lewis and his life, including well-known Lewis landmarks. It had been a difficult year after the accident that took her parents' lives, and, more than once, she had secretly wished for a wardrobe of her own that would transport her to another world. Being in this place years later made her feel as though she could connect to the stories in a way she never had before.

The inside of the pub was as unassuming as the exterior. Had one not known the unique heritage the walls held, it could be entirely overlooked. Mark spoke with the hostess about his reservation while Sadie drank in the details of the room, trying her best to commit each one to memory. Across the beam overhead was a hand painted quote by Lewis. It read, "My happiest hours are spent with three or four friends in old clothes tramping together and putting up in small pubs." In this moment, Sadie felt that sentiment at her core. She felt a deep happiness at being tucked into a corner booth with new friends in this hidden gem of a pub.

As an extra special bonus Mark had arranged for them to eat in the Rabbit Room, a corner of the establishment that housed several mementos from the Inklings. Once again, Sadie found herself snapping pictures and relishing the connection she felt with the past. Menus were passed around, and they all settled on ordering classic British fish and chips. When it arrived, Sadie found large cuts of deep-fried potatoes and a huge, singular piece of battered fish all wrapped in newspaper. The fish was missing its head, but its tail and some skin remained. She and Mark spent a good portion of the time comparing the meal to its Canadian counterparts. Bridget was especially interested since she had never eaten the Canadian version of the dish. Sadie liked these chips better than the ones she had spent hours slinging at Freddy's, but she preferred it when her fish didn't look as though it had just been pulled out of the water.

Mark took a slurp of his soda and wiped his mouth with a napkin. "Did our mother like to travel?" he asked.

Sadie thought about the question. "I think so. She travelled a lot before I was born. After that most of our trips were to visit family in other provinces. I think that they always had plans to do more, but between her work schedule and my school schedule there wasn't much time for taking big trips like this."

"I bet she would love to be here with you."

A familiar sadness washed over Sadie. It was one more thing that she would never be able to share with her parents. She wondered what they would think of her being here with Mark and Bridget. Would they approve of them forming a relationship? Surely they would be pleased to know that they had found each other after all this time. Wouldn't they? She would never really know for certain.

Bridget must have noticed the dark cloud that enveloped Sadie because she elbowed her husband in the stomach.

He caught the hint and apologized. "I'm sorry. I shouldn't have brought that up. I didn't mean to put a damper on your day. We can talk about something else."

"It's okay. It sometimes just catches me off guard, you know. There's so much that I wish they could be a part of, so much of my life that I wish they could see. You're right, though. She would have loved this. All of it. They both would have."

Bridget reached across the table and squeezed Sadie's hand. Her bright blue eyes softened with a look of sincere tenderness. "I am sure that both your parents would be very proud of you and the woman you are becoming. Allow yourself to feel however you need to. This day is about you."

"Thanks. I think I just need a moment." She excused herself from the table and headed for the loo. In the privacy of the tiny room, Sadie allowed the tears to fall. This was not the way it was supposed to happen. Grief was not supposed to follow her here. She braced herself on the sink and stared at her reflection in the small, gilded mirror on the wall above it. The eyes of the young woman staring back at her were familiar. Her expression wore a familiar mask, one that she used to pretend that life was good and easy and that everything was fine. But she could feel a shift. Every day it felt like more and more cracks were appearing in that mask making it harder to keep up the façade. Sadie took a deep breath and willed herself to keep it together. This was not the time nor the place to fall apart. She splashed some cold water on her face and, lifting her wavy tresses with one hand, pressed the cool palm of her other on the base of her neck. *You can do this, Sadie. Pull it together.*

Her internal pep talk was interrupted by a light tap on the door. "Are you okay, Sadie?" Bridget asked from outside the door.

"Yes," she called out. "Just finishing up." Sadie checked her reflection one last time before pasting a smile back on her face and opening the door to a very concerned looking Bridget.

"I'm so sorry about that. Mark didn't mean to upset you. He tends to be pretty direct, which I love, but it can be a little jarring at times if you are not used to it."

It had been a similar story for much of her life. Some well-intentioned person would say or do something that triggered her grief response. Thankfully, after all this time, Sadie had become a pro at pulling herself together and acting as if everything was fine, leaving the pain to be dealt with at another time. She flashed Bridget a toothy smile and, with all the confidence she could muster, replied "It's all good. I just needed to take quick 'loo' break before we headed out again. I'm ready now."

Bridget gave her a concerned look but said nothing more. They settled their tab and bid adieu to the darling little hideaway eatery. Sadie stood a moment in the door frame, allowing herself to soak in the fact that some of the greatest writers of all time had likely stood in this exact spot. It was a weird feeling, commemorating men who no longer dined in pubs or walked these streets. Men whose words were their legacy. For her parents, there were no immortalized words to commemorate them. For her parents, she was their primary legacy. The weight of that thought fell heavy on her shoulders.

They strolled through the town at a more leisurely pace this time, exploring side streets and unique architecture. Cobblestone, as it turns out, is far more challenging to walk on than one would initially believe. The uneven turf made Sadie grateful she had opted for sneakers instead of sandals. Her feet were already loudly protesting, and it was only midday.

As they passed by a quaint souvenir shop, Sadie paused in front of the wide, glass window, a giggle bubbling up from a happy place in her heart. There on display was a tiny Prince William bobblehead. She had to have it. It would be the perfect souvenir for boy-crazy Dawn. Mark and Bridget waited outside the shop while she poked inside, hoping that the cost of the trinket wouldn't be astronomical.

Sadie picked up tiny William and held him at eye level. "Do you want to travel to Canada?" she asked as she tapped his nose playfully. The head nodded vigorously. "That settles it then."

She placed the figurine on the counter in front of a teenaged young lady who seemed entirely disinterested in her role. "That'll be sixteen quid," the cashier said flatly.

Sadie was confused. "Quid? I, um, I…" she fumbled through her wallet, panic rising. All her money had been changed into pounds. How much was a quid? She was almost certain that there was nothing in her wallet that read "quid." Even still, she pulled out several bills and thumbed through them, desperately hoping that something would jump out at her.

Other customers had lined up behind her now, adding to the rising sense of panic. The cashier was just staring at her blankly, offering no further explanation, when she felt a gentle tap on her shoulder. It was an elderly lady who simply pointed to the twenty-pound bill that was in her hand. Sadie laid it on the counter and thanked the lady for her help. The woman nodded and then gestured to the cashier who was extending Sadie's change and package. She took them, kept her head down, and made her exit from the store as quickly as she could, nearly colliding into Mark as she did.

"Whoa, what's the hurry?" Mark said as he caught his balance.

"Sorry. I needed to get out of there before I embarrassed myself anymore. What in the world is a quid? I thought your money was in pounds."

Bridget and Mark looked at each other and smiled but didn't laugh at Sadie's innocent question. Mark turned to keep walking through town as he offered an explanation. "A quid is a pound, it's just a slang term. It's kind of like bucks and dollars."

"Oh. Well, that is helpful to know." She sighed and sat down on a newly vacated bench. "I am a colossal train wreck at this travel abroad thing. Do you think I will ever get the hang of it here?"

Mark sat next to her and "Absolutely. You have only been here a week. Don't be so hard on yourself. It's a completely different culture."

He was right, of course. Still, Sadie couldn't help but to feel discouraged by the ineptitude. How could she expect to travel the world if she couldn't even manage to take a picture or buy a silly bobblehead without incident.

"It won't help to dwell on it. That will just make it feel worse than it is. Let's keep going. There's so much more to see," Mark said encouragingly.

And see they did. The remainder of the day was filled to the brim. They walked through churches, browsed shops, toured more colleges, and ate delicious treats. Mark wanted to push the day until the last train, but Sadie's feet loudly protested any more walking. By dusk, she was completely tapped out and anxious for any position that would keep her feet off the ground.

The train ride back into Chipping Norton was quiet. It had been a very full day of walking, eating, touring, and taking dozens of pictures, and they were all exhausted. Sadie leaned against the window and scrolled through the photos on her phone, mentally reliving the highlight reel. It had certainly been more of an emotional rollercoaster than she had anticipated. There had been several magical moments where Sadie felt as though she had been placed right in the middle of one of her novels. And yet, there were also several moments when she had felt completely overwhelmed with her own shortcomings and her inability to be free from the past. She had not expected that her confidence to take on new experiences would be so shaken.

She paused her photo scrolling on a picture of the door into Regent's Park College and smiled to herself. For evermore, Sadie would think of that door as a metaphor for the city. The true treasure of Oxford was not in the grandiose and lofty and elaborate. The true treasure of the city was in the secret, hidden wonders. Those places that are meant for someone to quietly discover and unwrap as a beautiful gift meant just for them—the secret doors, the tucked away places, the hidden delights. Those are the things that Sadie treasured. Those were the moments that she would hold in her heart. It was no wonder that C.S. Lewis could imagine a world where a simple wardrobe could become a gateway to a world of wonder. Today Sadie had discovered her own wardrobe to a magical land, and it thrilled her all the way to her toes.

Chapter Fourteen

It had been several days since their Oxford adventure and life had fallen into a natural rhythm for the four of them. While Mark worked during the days, Sadie, Bridget, and Lily would hop the train in the morning and head to visit local towns and shops along the Cotswolds. They were always back by Lily's nap time and would spend the afternoon reading or chatting or prepping for dinner. The evenings were typically a stroll through town or a patio party, as Lily called it, where they would gather around the outside table and play games or read stories. It was Lily's favourite time of the day, and Sadie could understand why. It was the simple pleasure of leisure time together with her family. Sadie could remember those kinds of moments with her own parents. They were some of the best.

One such evening at the Burgess' home when she was enjoying time with her newly found family, Sadie finally mustered the courage to pull out the photo album that she had safely tucked into the bottom of her suitcase. Its pages held snapshots of her parents, forever frozen in time. She had packed it knowing that, for Mark, these images would be a window into his mother, perhaps the only real one he might have. However, deciding to share them was difficult, not because they would make her sad. No, she had poured over these images so often that they were embedded in her memory. It was difficult because it meant that she was truly sharing her mother with another person.

In every way, though, Mark had proven himself to her. He deserved to know the woman who had birthed him. He deserved to know just how wonderful she was. And so, under the lamp light in the corner of the living room one evening, Mark and Sadie together poured over the images. He asked questions. She shared stories. They both cried. It was a healing time for them.

One picture in particular caught Mark's attention. Sadie remembered the day it was taken. They had just finished a board game where her mom had been certain she would trump her dad, but when they tallied the scores, he had beat her by only a few points. Mom was sour and Dad teased her mercilessly about it. She had held her face in a pretend scowl until Dad started tickling her to make her laugh. She couldn't help herself as she caved in with a deep belly giggle. Dad grabbed his camera and snapped a picture of her, saying that he always wanted to remember the way she looked in that exact moment.

Sadie could understand why the photo fascinated Mark. Her cheeks were flushed, her hair was mussed, and her eyes twinkled with the light of laughter. But it was her smile and the way she held her head that made her look exactly like a mirror image of Mark. The similarities between them in that photo were startling.

"Keep it," Sadie had found herself saying.

"Are you sure?" he asked.

"Yes. You look just like her in this one. Besides, I have all these committed to memory anyway. Take it."

Watching him gingerly slip the photo out of its sleeve and place it on their mantel, Sadie knew that she had made the right decision in sharing this album with him. It felt good to know that her mother's memory was being treasured by another heart.

They hadn't talked about her parents again since that night, and Sadie was grateful for that. Each conversation, though positive, was emotionally taxing. She was enjoying simply being in their world.

On this particular day, Mark was working in London, so he planned to be home late. The weather was overcast, and the dense, and gray clouds filled the sky, carrying with them the promise of rain. As a result, Sadie and Bridget had opted to stay closer to home and had instead taken Lily for an early walk before picking up a few necessities at the local grocer. The three then spent the remainder of the morning playing on the floor of the living space while the rain danced across the roof providing a rhythmic soundtrack to their play. The slower pace of the day had been nice for a change. It had given Sadie a chance to do some laundry, catch up on her journaling, and respond to messages from back home. She even took time to handwrite notes on postcards to mail to Dawn and Lynn and Jack. On the front of each postcard was a picture of an iconic red phone booth, each in a different locale. Sadie thought the postcards were adorable.

Even though there was probably no way that the postcards would make it home before she did, she at least wanted to try. Her family would get a kick out of international mail. Not to mention the fact that taking a walk downtown to the post office was appealing for other reasons. She appreciated all that the family was doing to make her feel welcome, and she loved spending time with them especially because they were the entire reason she was here, but she had spent little time alone since she had landed. The adventurer in her was itching to explore on her own, at her own pace, through her own eyes.

It was late afternoon once the rain cleared. She stepped outside and took a deep breath of the fresh earthy scent of wet grass and soil. Sadie had always marveled at the fact that rain—something that had no smell or taste or colour in and of itself—could cause the world to come alive and respond so vibrantly. The post office was only a short walk from their home, and even though the day carried with it an overall dreariness, Sadie walked with a skip in her step. The adventure watered a seedling of hope in her spirit like the rain watered the ground. Here she was walking the streets of a quaint little European town on her own. She was a capable and confident young woman with a world of possibility unfolding before her. If only Tom could see her now, he would see that she didn't need his approval or his God to be happy.

The process to mail her postcards was simple: a few stamps and air mail stickers and they were off on their own journey across the pond. Stepping out of the post office, Sadie was hit with wafting smells of deep-fried foods that made her mouth water. They seemed to be coming from a local pub at the corner named The Royal Oak. It was nearing dinnertime, and her stomach began to grumble at the savoury scents. Sadie had told Bridget not to expect her back until later, so she opted to duck into the pub to experience some of the local fare. To her delight, a musician was set up in the corner belting out a rousing diddy. It was a different kind of music than the sea shanties she might hear in the pubs in Lunenburg, but it was toe-tapping all the same.

She followed the hostess to an empty table along the back of the room. It was a cozy little corner and if she angled her chair just right, she would have a clear view of the performer, a mid-thirties hipster with a long beard, cabbie hat, and tattered jacket. He was perched on a stool with an acoustic guitar on his lap and a harmonica positioned in front of his mouth by a metal holder around his neck. Sadie reveled in the small victory of feeling very much like a mature, seasoned traveler who was confident enough in herself to dine alone and appreciate the local culture.

Graciously accepting the menu, she browsed through the assortment of enticing dishes. When the server arrived at the table to take her order, in typical fashion Sadie was still undecided. She quickly opted for bangers and mash, primarily because it was the most "British" sounding food on the menu. *Though, I suppose everything on the menu is British when you're in Britain,* she chuckled to herself.

Settling into the seat she focused her attention on the musician at the microphone just as an attractive young man slipped into the seat across from her.

"Now what's a lush little thing like you doing sittin' all alone?" he said flirtatiously. The young stranger leaned back in the chair, giving no indication that he intended to leave.

Sadie was completely taken aback. Never had a guy been so brazen with her. He was smooth, she'd give him that, and his accent made him all-the-more appealing. It was clear that he was the type of guy who was used to getting his way. She guessed that he had to be at least twenty-two, perhaps a little older. The stubble along his square jawline boasted a maturity that seemed beyond the teenage years. Blond hair curled across his forehead and ocean blue eyes full of amusement dared her to respond. His broad-lipped grin and cocked eyebrows conveyed an arrogance that undercut any natural appeal he might have carried.

"I'm enjoying the music, if you must know." Sadie did her best to match his level of confidence, but internally she was feeling more and more uncomfortable. Her voice came out wobblier than she would have liked.

"Oh, an American. We don't get too many Americans around here. What's your name?"

Why does everyone automatically assume I'm American? "Canadian, actually," she corrected. "And it's Sadie."

He didn't notice the correction and continued his pitch. "Well Sadie, this place is not bad, but what say you and I blow this joint, and I show you how Brits can really party."

Before she could find a way to refuse, two more guys about the same age sauntered over to her table. One with bright red hair and a long peacoat clapped her seatmate on the shoulder and jerked his thumb in her direction. "Who's your friend, Oliver, and where can we find one?"

Oliver laughed. "This is Sadie. Sadie, my mates Chuck and Thomas." He gestured first to the young man with the red hair and then to the other who was shorter in stature with slicked dark brown hair and dark set eyes. The friends were now pulling chairs up to her table and Sadie felt panic rising in her chest at how quickly she seemed to be losing control of the situation. "Don't make yourselves too comfortable boys,

Sadie and I were just about to head off so I can show her a good time. Maybe I'll find out if Americans are as wild as they say."

"Actually," Sadie responded slowly, disgusted at the lewd comment and the arrogant way they spoke about her as if she were not in the room, "I'm not going anywhere with anyone. And, as I already told you, I am Canadian, thank you very much." She crossed her arms for emphasis and gave them a level stare.

"Ohh...you've found a lively one," Thomas said, punching Oliver in the arm.

"You know I always did love a good challenge." He winked at her and Sadie's insides twisted in panic as she realized they would not be so easily deterred. Immediately her brain began to rapid-fire possible outcomes of the situation and none of them were good. It was all newspaper headlines and breaking stories kind of bad.

Nervously, she scanned the room desperate to find some form of escape. The restroom seemed to be the most reasonable option. She could hide out there until they got bored of her and left. Before she could find a way to excuse herself, she felt someone approach behind her.

A familiar sounding, no-nonsense voice growled at the boys. "Sod off, Oliver, and take your mates with you. You've got no business causing trouble around here."

"Geez, Pia. Don't get your knickers in a twist. We were just being neighbourly."

"I believe it's time to take your welcoming party elsewhere, unless of course you would like me to ring up your father."

Oliver held his hands up in surrender and pushed back from the table. "No cause for anything drastic. We're leaving." He gave Sadie a coy grin and laid a small rectangular card on the table. "If you change your mind and want a real tour guide, give me a ring." The three young men left the pub without any further incident, but it wasn't until the door closed behind them that Sadie exhaled a breath she didn't realize she had been holding.

Her rescuer sat down in the now vacant seat across from Sadie. The voice belonged to Pia, the kind woman with the wild red curls. "You alright, dearie?" she asked.

"Thank you for that. I…I'm…" Sadie's voice cracked. As relief washed away the momentary fear, hot angry tears escaped and cascaded down her cheeks. Even though nothing had happened, she felt violated. She buried her face in her hands, overwhelmed with the situation.

"I'm such a loser," Sadie huffed as she succumbed to self-pity. "I can't do anything right here."

"Come now. Don't be talking like that." Pia swiped a hand across the air as if to bat away the negative thought. "We do not wear sacks of shame. We adorn ourselves with garments of grace. Oliver and his pals are trouble and have been since they were pups. I've had to throw them out of my place a couple times now for causing a stir. You've done nothing wrong."

"Maybe not, but it's just further proof that I'm a mess. I'm just not cut out for all this."

Pia reached across the table and squeezed her hand. "Tell me about it."

It wasn't said as a demand, but rather an invitation. There was something about Pia that felt safe, as though her presence had more than once provided balm to a troubled soul. Before she could stop herself,

Sadie was pouring her heart out to the woman. She left nothing out. Oliver, the embarrassing moments she had endured since landing, her new relationship with Mark, the grief that seemed to follow her even here. She even spilled about Tom and their blowout just before she left.

Pia listened intently, her face revealing no surprise or judgement. When Sadie had said all that there was to say, her cheeks began to flush with embarrassment at her verbal diarrhea. Pia was practically a stranger, and Sadie had just confessed her innermost struggles to her. *Oh well, there's nothing I can do about it now.* She looked sheepishly at the woman across from her, hoping to at least glean from her some sage advice. Pia smiled tenderly but said nothing.

When the silence was nearing awkward, Pia finally spoke. "Feel better?"

Sadie thought about it. In spite of the weariness she felt after the emotional purge, her heart felt lighter and less burdened than it had in weeks. She nodded in response.

"Sometimes," Pia paused for emphasis, "yes, sometimes, healing is accessed by simply sharing our heart hurts with another and being heard."

Sadie wasn't completely convinced, but she allowed Pia to continue.

"You have been carrying a lot my dear. We are not made to hold such things inside. We are not failures in allowing others to help lift those burdens. Quite the opposite. I think that you will find that the good stuff of life comes when we journey together rather than trying to figure it all out alone." She paused again. "So, this trip hasn't been all that you hoped it would be." It was said as more of a question than a statement.

Sadie stared at her hands. "You know, Mark and Bridget have been so lovely, and I have gotten to see and do some incredible things. It's just that I have spent most of my life dreaming of getting out of my small town and seeing the world. Of finally being known for something other than my past. I guess I just had this picture in my head of how great of a world traveler I would be. After everything that's happened since I landed, I feel as though it would be better if I stayed at home. Every time I feel a glimpse of confidence in myself and my decisions, I do something stupid. Or I made a poor judgement call. Or I lose control of my emotions."

Pia once more reached across the table and patted Sadie's hand sympathetically. "You think you're the only one that makes mistakes, the only one who has embarrassed themselves? Or…" she narrowed her eyes at Sadie, "the only one who has tried to run from their past? It is a part of life. We all struggle from time to time. The brave ones are those who are willing to make mistakes, pick themselves up, and keep going."

"But," she leaned in close and lowered her voice as though imparting some precious secret. "Do not be fooled by the world's empty promises, dearie. Running away will never be the answer. You cannot hide from your past any more than you can hide an elephant in a pig pen. It is a part of you, a part of your story that has shaped you, however painful it may be. Where you come from, the people who know your story and love you for all the parts of it, that is something not to take for granted. You need wings, but you also need roots."

Chapter Fifteen

Pia's words were still imprinted on her mind and heart when she woke the next day. Sadie hadn't made the connection at the time, but much of what Pia had said was an echo of the valedictory speech Sadie had given only a few short weeks earlier about not letting the fear of failure keep you from taking chances. Apparently, it was much easier to dole out life lessons than to live them. While Pia's advice had not been what Sadie expected to hear, she had to admit that after talking with her, she felt better. As for needing roots, she was not quite ready to embrace those in Lunenburg, but the conversation had certainly given her pause. There was a lot to consider.

After a quick breakfast, Sadie spent almost two hours recounting her adventures to Dawn. They had coordinated a facetime call to catch up on all the details since first landing because, as Dawn had said, "text messages simply weren't cutting it."

Sadie was grateful for the opportunity to honestly vent to someone who knew her completely and still loved her. Her emotions were still fairly raw after last evening's run in with Oliver and her surprising heart-to-heart with Pia. Pia had been right about the importance of sharing her burdens though. Sadie needed the type of comfort that can only be found by pouring over every detail with the most trusted of confidants, that and an extra large Cadbury sea salt and caramel chocolate bar, which she had been saving for just the right moment.

"This trip certainly has been full of ups and downs. I wish that you were here." She snapped off a piece of chocolate and let it melt on her tongue.

Dawn pouted dramatically. "Me too. I would have told that turd, Oliver, exactly what kind of low-life he is."

"I don't doubt it." Sadie flopped on her stomach across the bed, propped the phone up against a pillow, and lowered her voice so as not to be heard through the thin walls. "I know that Pia said that I need to pick myself up and keep going, but…" her voice trailed off.

"But what?" Dawn's impatience was evident.

"I don't know. I guess I'm still just shaken by that whole debacle."

"Seriously, who uses the word *debacle* anymore. You read too much. Forget Oliver and whatever other embarrassing things you've done. I think you're just still wound too tightly after all the exam-graduation-Tom stuff. You need to get out and let your hair down. Have some fun."

"You're probably right. Today might be just what I need. Bridget has arranged to take me out to a special place for tea. Mark offered to watch Lily because he said it was more of a ladies' outing. From the sounds of it, I'll need to be fancier than just jeans and sneakers."

"Not exactly what I was thinking, but sure. Will that be weird though?" Dawn asked. "Like aren't you supposed to be there to spend time with your brother, not his wife?"

Leave it to Dawn to say exactly what she was thinking. Sadie admired that quality and more than once had wished for the ability to do the same. "Bridget is actually really great. I have ended up spending a lot of time with her and Lily because Mark still needs to work during the day. She's really easy to talk to though and I've been appreciating her friendship."

Dawn cocked one eyebrow and made a face. "Just as long as you remember that the position of best friend is already filled."

Sadie laughed out loud, which felt good. Dawn was good for her soul. "Don't worry. There's no one in the world that could replace you. Talk soon." She tapped her nose twice and pointed at her friend. Dawn repeated the gesture back and signed off. Since second grade under the shade of the tube slide that had been their version of a secret handshake. It meant 'We're a team. I've got your back.'

Sadie rifled through her suitcase and pulled out the one dress that she had thought to pack at the last minute. It was slightly crumpled from being neglected at the bottom of her bag. She laid the navy dress across the bed and smoothed it out with her hands. While she wasn't the type to wear dresses often, this was one of her favourites. The hem of the full skirt and the neckline were embroidered with delicate flowers. A pleated bodice and soft bubble sleeves capped off the dress. Sadie liked to imagine that Anne Shirley would approve of the puffiness of these sleeves.

Looking in the mirror, Sadie felt pleased at her appearance. Her hair was partly pinned back allowing some of her curly tresses to rest on her shoulders. The dress made her feel a little buoyant and feminine. She knew she couldn't compare to Bridget's flawless beauty, but at this moment, she was pleased with the person staring back at her in the mirror. Fingering the gold locket around her neck, Sadie wondered if she would be able to keep her thoughts and emotions in check. There certainly seemed to be a lot bubbling just below the surface, more so lately than usual, no doubt caused by the fact that she'd been forced to relive much of the past since meeting Mark. Taking a slow breath, Sadie determined that today would be everything Dawn said she needed. It would be fun and light and relaxing. One quick dab of lip gloss and she was out the door.

The day was overcast, but the air was warm. Sadie had brought a sweater with her, just in case, having quickly learned about the unpredictable nature of British weather. A short train ride brought the two companions to a neighbouring town surrounded by sprawling English countryside. Bridget looked like the cat that ate the canary the whole trip. She had refused to give Sadie much detail about the excursion, indulging only that this would be a unique experience for them both.

"I have only heard of this place from friends and never been to it myself, which makes today even more special. It comes very highly recommended. Thank you for sharing this with me, Sadie."

"Of course. Thanks for planning this for us," Sadie responded. "But, you know, I'd be even more grateful if I knew what exactly *this* is going to be." She cocked an eyebrow at Bridget as they alighted from the train, hoping that she might offer up more information. Bridget, however, merely smiled and waved down a taxicab.

The cab driver was an older gentleman with an accent so thick that Sadie could barely understand a word he was saying.

"To Secret Cottage, please," Bridget said politely to the man. He nodded and turned the car into the street. She leaned over to Sadie and in a lowered voice said, "See, I told you it was secret."

Staring out the window of the cab, Sadie allowed herself to be transported. The landscape was so quaint and picturesque that she felt as though she were in a different era entirely.

The car turned down a winding lane flanked with lush meadows and stopped in front of an average sized thatched roof cottage. A smartly dressed, middle-aged woman met them at the door. "Welcome to Secret Cottage. My name is Becky. This cottage and the grounds on which it sits have been in my family for over three hundred years. We have loved it so much that my husband and I decided several years ago to share our home with others by opening it up as a historical site and tea house. If you'll follow me, I will show you around. Please do not hesitate to ask any questions."

Stepping inside the cottage, Sadie was impressed with the blend of new and old. While the main living areas were outfitted with modern features, like lights and appliances, most of the architecture was preserved as one would have found it several decades ago. Large weathered wooden beams lined the low ceiling. Those and the small carved doorways made the home feel quaint and cozy. But the charm of the place was found in the special touches that were a testament to one gifted in making a house a home: the handmade quilt was neatly draped over a claw-footed armchair; the display of antique bottles and jars were mounted above the stove; the watercolour paintings of wildflowers adorned the walls. Sadie took her time walking through the space. She wanted to appreciate every detail.

The true "secret" of the cottage, however, lied in vibrant and elaborate gardens which sprawled across the grassy grounds. Sadie let the beauty ignite her senses. It was remarkable, both in the vivid display of colour and the sweet and earthy aromas. Neatly trimmed hedges framed in a sea of purple violets and white peonies. Hearty, pink hydrangea bushes buzzed to life as bumblebees worked to harvest the abundance of pollen. Hollyhocks stood almost as tall as Sadie as they stretched their pink and purple blooms to the sky. In the center of the garden a wooden trellis stood covered in creeping, purple wisteria.

As she listened to Becky describe the pains taken to cultivate the lush foliage, she could not help but think back to a poem they had recently studied in English class by the famous writer Rudyard Kipling—"The Glory of the Garden." Sadie couldn't remember exactly how the poem went, but did remember one stanza which had stood out enough for her to commit it to memory:

> Our England is a garden, and such gardens are not made
> By singing: "Oh, how beautiful," and sitting in the shade
> While better men than we go out and start their working lives.
> At grubbing weeds from gravel-paths with broken dinner-knives.

Kipling had been using the garden as a metaphor to refer to the formation of their country and the role that each person played in that, but it still fit. No garden or civilization or anything of beauty was created without hard work. Sadie wondered just exactly what garden she had been tending with all the hard work she had done over the past few years.

Becky escorted she and Bridget to a long table covered with a crisp white linen cloth in the center of the garden. Large wooden chairs flanked the table and were decorated with colourful throw pillows. The chairs were a statement piece, looking as though they had been handcrafted by a skilled carpenter. Running her thumb along the intricate floral carvings on the armrest, Sadie was once again impressed at the attention to detail.

Becky handed them each a simple white card on which were listed a wide assortment of teas and requested their orders. Sadie was hesitant to sample any of the unfamiliar brews and so settled on a classic mint tea while Bridget selected an Earl Grey. With a nod, Becky excused herself and slipped back into the cottage.

A leafy canopy of trees shaded them from the midday sun, which occasionally nosed through the clouds. For several minutes, no one spoke as they each digested the beauty of their surroundings. Bridget was the first to break the silence.

"It really means a lot that you would take the time to come with me today, Sadie. I know your time here is short. I must confess, that I do have an ulterior motive in bringing you out here."

Sadie adjusted her position so that she was facing her friend. What motive could Bridget possibly have? Hadn't they been together the past two weeks?

"I wanted to be able to talk freely without Mark or Lily around. I do love our home, but it doesn't lend itself well to private conversations."

Once more Bridget had piqued her interest. What private conversation did they need to have that she didn't want overheard? *Did I do something to offend her? I wouldn't be surprised the way my luck is going,* Sadie thought. "What did you want to talk about?"

At that moment, they were interrupted by Becky who placed in front of each of them a small teapot, teacup, and saucer. Unlike at Elora's Café, the fine bone China sets were all matching in their delicate design—a floral pattern trimmed in gold.

Once they were alone again, Bridget continued. "Well, not something so much to talk about, but rather something to tell you." In that moment Bridget's lit up with an expression of pure glee. "I'm pregnant!" she finally blurted, her hands resting lovingly on her stomach.

"You are? That's fantastic!" Sadie exclaimed, her surprise masking the relief she felt at not being at fault for something. She jumped up and enthusiastically ran around the long table to envelop her friend in a congratulatory hug. "I can't believe it. I'm hugging both of you," she giggled at the happy thought. Bridget's eyes glistened with tears of joy.

New life. What a fitting place to celebrate such news. The two exchanged one more loving squeeze before composing themselves and serving themselves tea.

As Bridget demurely sipped her tea, she continued with her confession. "The only thing is that I haven't told Mark yet." Sadie's face must have registered her surprise because she quickly added, "Not because I'm nervous about it. No, we've been trying for another child, but because I fudged up our first announcement."

Bridget set her teacup on the saucer and twirled one of her long tresses with her finger. "I had so many ideas about how it would all go, but I was so taken off guard. We had been trying for so long, and I had taken so many negative tests. When the test showed a faint second line, I was so uncertain and scared to actually hope that it might be positive. I froze. I sat on the floor completely stupefied as to what to do. That's how Mark found me." She laughed. "Ever the voice of reason, he took me to the doctor so that we could hear the news firsthand. So I just want to make this next announcement fun for him. Without the stress."

"I'm honoured that you would share all of this with me, but how do I play into it?" Sadie asked.

"I need your help. I'm not all that creative, so I was hoping you could help me come up with a fun way to tell him." Bridget folded her hands as though pleading and flashed her best puppy dog eyes. "Pretty please?"

Sadie laughed. It was fun to see this side of Bridget. Sadie was so glad that she had agreed to come on this adventure with her. This experience was exactly the type of thing she had dreamed of when she imagined travelling the world, and today, it was just the pick-me-up she needed. "Of course I will," she replied.

At that moment, Becky returned to their table carrying a three-tiered serving tray, each level held a different variety of delectable treats. As Sadie had learned early on in her trip, *tea* referred to the whole meal, not just the hot drink and she was excited to dive into these. Becky explained that they were to begin on the bottom with the selection of savoury finger sandwiches and pastries then move to the second tier of scones, jams, and clotted cream, and finish with the sweets on the top tier. It all looked divine.

"Enough about me," Bridget said between bites. "Tell me about you. I couldn't help but notice that when Lily brought up the topic of boyfriends the other day that your cheeks betrayed you a little. Might there be someone back home who holds your heart?"

The question caught Sadie off-guard. She had been intentionally working so hard avoid any deep self-reflection, especially today. But Bridget had been so open and honest with her, she felt compelled to open up about Tom.

"Well, there is this guy—"

"I knew it," Bridget interjected.

Reaching for a cucumber finger sandwich she nodded and continued. "His name is Tom. He's a year older than me and lobster fisherman right now, but he has plans to be a teacher."

"That sounds promising."

"It does. He likes to play baseball, he drives a beater pick-up truck, and he volunteers at his church youth group. We went on one date—our first and last," she added sourly.

"Oh no, what happened? He sounds like a catch—pun intended." Bridget chuckled at her own joke.

"I thought so too, but it turns out that he's a bit too self-righteous to want to actually date a heathen like me."

"Sadie, you are no heathen, lovey, let me assure you of that. Did he actually say that?"

"Well not exactly, but he did say that my unwillingness to submit my life to God was too big of an obstacle for us to overcome. He didn't want to get involved with me if we could not agree on matters of faith. Honestly, I was so angry that he would lead me on I could have thrown something at him."

Sadie braced herself expecting that Bridget would take Tom's side and tell her that she was off base about matters of faith, that Tom was right to end things. Bridget, however, said none of that. In fact, she offered no advice at all. She simply said, "That must have felt awful. Has he tried to talk to you since?"

"Yeah, he has texted a few times, but I never responded. Although he did like a couple of the pictures that I posted from this trip. What do you think that means?"

She shook her head as she spread clotted cream across one half of a scone. "No idea. I have long since tried to figure out men. I'm not even certain they know what they want half the time." Bridget paused, seeming to be conflicted on whether to say more.

Finally, she added, "Has Mark told you my faith story?"

Sadie shook her head.

"I only began a relationship with Jesus a few years ago. Well, six years to be exact, around the time that Mark and I had first met. In fact, it was primarily his influence that prompted me to make that decision."

Sadie was a surprised. She had assumed that Bridget had always been connected to the church considering the way that she carried herself and how passionate Bridget seemed to be about her faith. Sadie was especially intrigued by the fact that Mark was the catalyst for her change of heart. She couldn't ignore the parallels to her own situation. "I had no idea. What did Mark do?"

"He was an intern at the office in Oxford where I worked as a graphic designer. We ended up working closely together on a project. Our personalities were complimentary, and we became fast friends. He invited me to come with him church almost weekly, but I always politely refused. Church was ritualistic and formal. I had no issues with those who chose that path; I simply had no time for it."

Bridget smiled at the memory. "Mark was undeterred. He was always so kind and respectful when he would ask me to attend that I finally agreed. It was the best decision. His church was nothing like I has expected. Sure, there were traditional parts of the service, but the heart of it all caught me off-guard. A lovely woman spoke earnestly about Jesus and His love. I found myself moved to tears. It was a simple message, but one I had never heard. I am deeply and unconditionally loved by the God who created our universe. I decided that day to spend my life following that love. It has proven to be a good decision, and, as you know, one that has become the foundation of my relationship with Mark."

Sadie took a sip of her tea to allow her time to process before responding. Bridget's story was sincere and charming, much like her. Sadie appreciated her openness and wanted to be respectful of her friend, but honestly was not sure how to respond. The simple message of God's love was a nice thought, but her life was far more complicated than Bridget's seemed to be. She opted for steering the conversation in a safer direction. "You and Mark are a great couple. How long did you guys date?"

A light flush graced Bridget's cheeks. "That part may surprise you, but we actually only dated officially for about four months before he proposed."

"Really? Were you completely shocked by his proposal?"

"Yes and no. The proposal was a surprise to me, but we had already talked about marriage. We both just *knew* and when you are that confident, why wait?"

Sadie couldn't imagine being ready to marry someone after just four months, but then again, her relationship experience was limited. It seemed to have worked out for Mark and Bridget.

Bridget continued, "Thank you for letting me share all that about myself. But now I must know, for all your heartache, was Tom at least cute?"

Sadie sighed. "So cute. His eyes are like dark chocolate and he has this shaggy curly hair that makes him look both playful and rugged." Bridget nodded her understanding and gave her a knowing smile. Sadie knew that she could never replace Dawn but having a friend and confidant who was also family felt like a rare treat.

They were almost finished their tea when Becky reentered the yard escorting two silver-haired women clad in elaborate fascinator hats. They were seated at the opposite end of the long table, but immediately struck up conversation with the younger women.

The one in the purple hat spoke first. "G'day dears. I'm Eleanor. This is Hattie." She gestured toward her companion who ducked her head in greeting. "Lovely day for tea, isn't it?"

"Certainly. This is our first time here, and it has been delightful," responded Bridget.

"Isn't it though? The gardens are simply exquisite," Hattie replied.

Eleanor nodded vigorously in agreement, the feathers in her fascinator bobbing about as she did. "Yes, yes. Some of the finest that we have seen."

"What brings you to the Secret Cottage? Are you celebrating?" Sadie asked, secretly curious about their headdress.

"Well, we've been best friends since we were spring hens—" Eleanor started.

"Spring chickens," Hattie interrupted. "The phrase is spring chickens, not hens."

"Yes, yes. Spring chickens. That's what I meant. But our lives took us to different parts of the country and kept us busy. Raising babies is no small feat, you know. It was difficult to see each other as much as we would have liked, so we made a promise to meet every summer for a special tea and spend the whole day together chatting about anything and everything."

Hattie took over the explanation. "We were few years into our annual meetups when we decided that these times together were—"

"Special." Eleanor chimed in.

"Right. A celebration, if you will."

"Yes, yes," Eleanor interjected again. "And those who are celebrating must dress accordingly. So, we bought some of the finest fascinators that we could find and have worn them proudly on each of our visits, like today."

Eleanor was clearly the more talkative of the two, but Hattie the more proper. The way they bantered back and forth made Sadie a little dizzy, and the way the feathers on their head bobbed when they talked made them resemble spring chickens, but their sweetness was contagious. She could not help but smile.

They ladies looked as they were about to turn their attention back to each other when Eleanor wanted to add one more thought. "You know, it may not always be easy, but it is always worth it to put in the effort for someone that you care about."

"And it is always important to make each moment with someone you love a celebration," Hattie added. Seemingly content with the wisdom bestowed on the younger generation, Eleanor and Hattie turned to face each other once again. Their laughter and constant conversation a testament to the deep friendship that they shared.

Bridget and Sadie watched them for a moment before they finished up their own celebration. As they bid adieu to the two ladies and walked to meet their awaiting cab, Sadie was certain that they were characters she would not soon forget.

"Before we head to the train station, will you indulge me in one quick stop?" Bridget asked.

"Of course," Sadie responded. "Where did you need to go?"

"I believe a quick visit to the local millinery is in order. We need to buy some hats."

Chapter Sixteen

It was hard to believe that in only five short days she would be boarding a flight back to Nova Scotia. Sadie was still reeling a little from the fact that Bridget had entrusted her with the news of their pregnancy. Even now, she felt giddy at the secret, though she was nervous that Mark would not be happy that she knew before he did. Hopefully their plan to surprise him would make up for it. The whole train ride home yesterday the two had discussed potential ways to pop the news to Mark. They finally settled on a cute "Big Sister" shirt for Lily. It would be a sweet way to include their daughter in the surprise. Bridget was even able to order it online and have it delivered right away, which worked out well because she was understandably anxious to share the news with her doting husband.

While Bridget excitedly planned her pregnancy reveal, Sadie was meticulously planning her final farewell to England. She, Mark, and Bridget had decided together to save touring London until the end of the trip since she would be flying out of Heathrow anyway. It was the perfect plan and the ideal way to cap off her stay. Mark was going to take off a day of work so they would have two full days in the city before her flight on Sunday. Lily was going to stay with her grandparents again, which she was thrilled about. Sadie had the impression that they doted on their darling granddaughter. But then again, how could anyone not dote on Lily?

Bridget reached for her phone and looked at the caller. "It's mum." She answered the call and gestured that she was going to take it in the other room leaving Sadie and Lily on the living room floor—Sadie with her laptop and Lily with her dolls.

Bridget returned several minutes later, looking slightly distraught. "Well, that's unfortunate. Mum is under the weather. She's not going to be able to watch Lily tomorrow while I am at my pottery class. Looks like I'll have to miss." Mark had gifted Bridget pottery classes for her most recent birthday since it was something she had always wanted to learn. Part of the gift had been that her parents would step in to watch Lily, giving her some much needed time to herself. Her first class was supposed to start the next morning.

"No, don't do that. There's no need for you to miss your class," Sadie said. "I can watch her for you. Please, it's the least that I can do for all the hospitality that you've shown me. Besides, I would love to have some special time with her before I leave on Sunday."

Bridget thought about it for a moment, chewing on her bottom lip. "Are you sure? It wouldn't be for more than a couple of hours."

"Absolutely. We'll have so much fun together, won't we, Lily?" Sadie directed the question at the tiny tot who was now intently lining up each of her dolls end to end.

Lily looked up at her and nodded with a sweet smile. "I love Auntie Sadie." Sadie's heart warmed at the title.

"Well, alright. But only if you're sure you don't mind."

"Of course not. I'll be looking forward to it."

Bridget turned as if to head to the kitchen and then paused. "You know, Sadie, it has been really lovely having you with us these past couple weeks. You have become a dear friend, and I hope that you have felt loved and accepted here. We have been praying that you feel at peace. I'm sure that it hasn't always been an easy journey to relive your past, but for Mark's sake, for all of ours, I am so grateful that you have." Bridget spoke from a place of sweet sincerity and openness. Her words were like balm to Sadie's soul, soothing the raw emotions that had been repeatedly laid bare.

Sadie wanted to respond with the same kind of grace and honesty that Bridget had, but her words caught in her throat as tears threatened to spill out. Bridget seemed to sense Sadie's heightened emotions and took two graceful strides across the room, knelt, and wrapped her new-found sister-in-law in an understanding embrace.

"Thank you," Sadie whispered.

Bridget stood and gave Sadie a smile that said she understood her at a heart level. She left the two of them and fixed them all a lunch of cheese toasties and carrot sticks.

They ate their lunch together in the backyard. Bridget and Sadie sitting on the steps with their plates balanced on their knees and Lily nibbling bites in between games of hopscotch on the large grey patio stones. They sipped cucumber water and chatted about nothing in particular. As they sat, the midday sun warmed Sadie's skin and brought a happiness to her soul. The shimmering summer sun always tended to brighten one's outlook on the world. This was a sweet, simple moment, and one she wanted to wrap up and tuck in her pocket to pull out on the dark and gloomy days.

Lily's ponytail danced and glimmered golden in the sunlight as she hopped across the chalk squares. She hummed a tune and did her best to hop from one to the next. Occasionally she would try to balance on one foot, but would wobble and fall to one side or the other. Undeterred, Lily hummed a tune and kept hopping. Sadie was impressed at the focus and determination shown by one so young. Lily stopped jumping and yawned.

"That's our cue," Bridget said, scooping the toddler up into her arms. "Nap time, lovey."

"But I'm not sleepy, Mummy."

"Of course not, but it is time for us to tuck your stuffies in for their nap." Bridget winked at Sadie and carried Lily inside.

While Lily napped and Bridget did some housework, Sadie opted to make the most of the sunshine since it seemed to be a rare occurrence here. Taking her journal to the backyard, she made a cozy nest on the wicker loveseat positioned against the fence. She sat sideways, propping a pillow behind her back for support and using her knees as a table.

Journaling, for Sadie, had been an on-again-off-again relationship. She liked the idea of pen to paper, but she tended to write more when inspiration struck then for the purpose of recording the details of every day. Today she wanted to write to remember. Something that Bridget had said earlier still echoed against the caverns of her soul.

PEACE. She wrote that word across the top of a new page.

They were still praying for peace. In that moment, Sadie could almost believe that it was possible. She could almost believe that God was benevolent. In a loopy cursive, Sadie made a list of all the things that had brought her peace today:

Bridget's friendship, sunshine, cheese toasties, hopscotch; toddler "I love yous," new babies

Tapping the pen to her chin, Sadie reread the list, then, feeling quite introspective, scrawled across the bottom of the page the question: "Where does peace come from?" She didn't know the answer but felt as though it was a worthwhile question to ponder.

Closing her journal, Sadie stretched and stifled a yawn. The warm sun was making her sleepy, and she was quite comfortable in her cozy perch so she decided there would be no harm in just resting her eyes for a moment. She was awoken what felt like only moments later by a tiny palm patting her face.

"Auntie Sadie," a little voice whispered. "Auntie Sadie, you're snoring."

Sadie opened her eyes to find herself staring into a darling little face that was remarkably close. So close that she could feel Lily's breath on her cheek. "Hi sweetie. You all done your nap?"

"Uh huh. Mummy said I could go play. Were you pretending to be a bear?"

Sadie sat up and wiped away a trickle of drool that had form at her mouth. Apparently, she had been asleep for longer than a moment. "Not intentionally, but I guess I fell asleep, huh?"

"Do you want to have a tea party with me?" Lily asked, her little hands folded together as though pleading with Sadie.

It was nearly impossible to refuse the child any request, especially considering that their time together was so limited. Sadie allowed herself to be led to Lily's room where a tiny table had already been elaborately set for "tea." Following Lily's instructions, Sadie donned a pink feather boa and plastic tiara before gingerly taking a seat on a miniature chair.

"My name is Lady Lily. You are Lady Sadie. This is Mr. Wobbles. Mr. Wobbles loves teatime. Don't you, Mr. Wobbles?" Lily directed the question at a large, stuffed flamingo that was perched on a chair to Sadie's right.

"Is that right, Mr. Wobbles?" Sadie said, joining into the game of make believe. "Can I pour you a cup?"

"Oh no, no, no," Lily chided, passing her a tray of plastic cookies. "You serve the biscuits. I pour the tea."

Sadie suppressed a giggle. Lily took her role as hostess seriously. "Of course, Lady Lily. Would you like one biscuit or two?"

For the better part of an hour, Sadie was a little girl again as she dined on imaginary tea and waltzed with a stuffed flamingo. And she couldn't have thought of a better way to spend an afternoon.

****

The day dawned beautiful as it hummed the tune of simple routine and daily life. Mark buzzed around the kitchen, grabbing breakfast, and packing his briefcase for the day. He was humming to himself. There was an added spring in his step this morning, likely connected to the news that he was going to be a father again.

Bridget had surprised him with the news last evening. After Mark returned home from work, Sadie had gone for a walk to give them some privacy as a family, but she was included in the celebratory meal at her return. Mark, thankfully, was not upset that he wasn't the first to know. In fact, he appreciated the thoughtfulness of the reveal and that Sadie had been a part of it all. He seemed to kiss his wife with extra gusto this morning as he headed out the door.

Lily sat at the table munching on cereal and playing with her stuffed moose, still in her princess PJs and tousled bed head. Bridget, already showered and prepped for her class, was now standing at the kitchen counter washing dishes.

Sadie loved that they were so comfortable allowing her into their routine but seeing them like this made her heart ache for her past. She could remember the days when the morning song in her childhood home was the same. The days of semi-rushed breakfast and morning chats and hurrying to get ready for the day. Those simple moments are insignificant until they are gone. Then those memories become gilded in gold—treasured and cherished. What Sadie wouldn't give to relieve one regular, mundane day with her parents.

She sighed audibly at the picture. Bridget looked up from the dishes with concern in her eyes. "Are you alright?" she asked.

"Oh, yes. Sorry. I didn't mean to sigh like that. I was just…appreciating all of this. Your everydays are so sweet and picture perfect."

"It certainly doesn't feel picture perfect, at least most of the time. In fact, it quite often feels very much the opposite. Having you here is good for us—for me. You help me to appreciate the moments that I might find frustrating or tiring."

"I'm glad for that. It is nice to be so lovingly included in your family's rhythms."

Bridget dried her hands on a towel. "On that note. Thank you again for being willing to watch Lily this morning. I really did not want to miss out on this class, especially since it's our first one."

"Hey, no problem. I'm looking forward to it. We don't have much more time together before I fly home."

Lily hopped down from her chair and skipped across the room. Slipping her tiny hand into Sadie's, she looked up at her with wide, pleading eyes and asked, "Auntie Sadie, will you please get me dressed for the day?"

Sadie looked at Bridget who simply shrugged. "If you're okay with it, it would be helpful. I have a couple errands I could run before heading to the pottery studio."

"Sure," Sadie agreed, finding it nearly impossible to refuse the pixie-like face that stared up at her.

"Great," Bridget said, gathering her things. "You'll find all her clothes in the chest of drawers in her room. She will be able to show you. Her hairbrush, hair bows, and toothbrush are all in the loo at the top of the stairs." She leaned over and kissed the top of Lily's head.

"You be a good girl for Auntie Sadie, alright lovey?"

"Yes, mummy. I will," she nodded her head so vigorously her whole body bounced.

Bridget left, leaving the two of them standing at the window waving goodbye. Sadie crouched down and looked into Lily's clear, blue eyes.

"We are going to have so much fun together. Should we go get ready first?"

Lily nodded and held out her arms to be carried. Sadie obliged and the two spent the next fifteen minutes finding just the right outfit, which, according to Lily, was an ensemble of pink on pink with a smattering of sparkle across her shirt and polka dots on her leggings. Sadie thought it best not to argue with the darling three-year-old who was so proud of the selection.

Doing Lily's hair was a nerve-wracking experience. The bedtime tangles needed to be brushed out, which required a little bit of effort, and Sadie wanted to be gentle with the little girl who was being very vocal when she pulled too hard. Eventually they emerged successful, if not slightly less polished than when Bridget was at the helm.

For almost two hours, the pair played with every toy that Lily owned. At least, that was how it felt to Sadie. Lily was relishing the fact that she had a personal playmate and so hopped from activity to activity. After their third time reading *The Velveteen Rabbit*, Sadie decided that some fresh air might be a nice change of pace before lunch. The early morning drizzle had dissipated, and the clouds were clearing. A little sunshine on their skin would be good for both of them.

Once they were outside, Lily quickly tired of the sidewalk chalk that Sadie had suggested they play with and decided that she wanted to ride her trike. It was still sitting outside from the last adventure she had taken, and so Sadie agreed.

"We aren't going to go too far though. Okay, Lily? We have to be back in time to get lunch ready." The Burgess' driveway was too small to provide any real space to bike, but after almost three weeks here, Sadie felt confident enough to make a loop around the neighbourhood without getting lost.

"Okay, Auntie," Lily agreed. She enthusiastically hopped onto the purple three-wheeler, her blond ponytail bouncing as she did. Foil ribbon fluttered from the handlebars as Lily pedaled circles around Sadie and sang a silly, made-up song. Turning onto the sidewalk the two headed in the direction of downtown. The sidewalk dipped down a steep hill and, before Sadie realized it, Lily started to coast ahead of her.

The next sixty seconds felt like an eternity.

As the houses on either side of them opened to a side street, another cyclist suddenly emerged from behind a building. The man was talking on a cell phone and too late noticed sweet Lily voraciously pedaling her purple chariot across the street. They collided, the force sending Lily flying off the bike backwards where she landed hard on her back. Sadie's stomach lurched as she watched, in slow motion, helpless, as Lily's fragile blond head ricocheted off the concrete.

Chapter Seventeen

Sadie rushed to Lily's side, careful not to move or jostle her.
"Lily?" Panic gripped Sadie's heart like a vice. There was no movement or response from the tiny body, no cries of pain. "Lily!" She yelled this time, desperation evident in her voice. *No! Please, God, no. Make her wake up. This can't be happening.*

The other biker had regained his footing and was now on Lily's other side. The tiny girl remained unresponsive as a small pool of blood seeped slowly from the back of her head. The sight made Sadie's stomach churn and her heart race faster. Across from her the young biker was crouched over Lily and already on his phone.

"I'm calling 999. She needs an ambulance immediately. Whatever you do, don't move her. This looks like a head injury." Outwardly, the man's voice was direct and controlled, but his hands were shaking, a betrayal that revealed the truth of his emotions.

Sadie nodded, her throat feeling like it was full of cotton. Panic had taken hold of her body and she felt the inability to think or rationalize clearly. She was grateful for the other person on the scene who was able to react quickly.

While they waited for the ambulance, Sadie gently held Lily's hand and begged God to protect her. There was nothing else that Sadie could do. She felt incredibly helpless. Seconds felt like hours. In the distance, a siren wail pierced the air and Sadie felt herself begin to breathe again.

"It's going to be alright now, Lily girl. They are going to take good care of you."

The young biker had remained silent as they waited, but he spoke to her now. "I am so sorry. I didn't see her." The words were strained and filled with remorse.

"It was an accident. It was no one's fault." Even as she said the words, Sadie knew that she didn't believe them. Someone was at fault— her. She should have insisted that Lily wear a helmet. She should have stayed right by Lily's side. How could she have been so irresponsible? Now, because of her, a precious little life might be hanging in the balance. Sadie thought she might be sick.

The paramedics arrived and worked quickly and calmly. They fitted her with a neck brace and hoisted Lily's tiny body onto the stretcher and into the back on the ambulance. Sadie sat at her side inside the truck, never letting go of the tiny hand. With her free hand, she pulled out her phone and called Bridget. She only prayed that they would be able to make it quickly to the hospital.

At the emergency room, Sadie was ushered to a waiting area as they wheeled Lily, still unconscious, through two large doors. Sitting was impossible so Sadie paced back and forth in the small area. *She's going to wake up. She's going to be fine. She just has to be,* Sadie thought.

Time seemed to crawl as she waited for any information on the status of the young girl. She had been waiting almost an hour when Mark and Bridget ran into the room. Sadie met them and the dam of her emotions gave way. Sobs rocked her as she buried her face in her hands. "I'm so sorry," she said through tears. "She wanted to ride her trike and she got ahead of me, and I didn't see the other biker in time."

Concern clouded the faces of both parents, but Mark spoke with calm authority. "It's not your fault, Sadie. Lily is in the hands of Jesus. We will trust Him with her."

At that moment, a middle-aged man clad in a white lab coat and carrying a clipboard entered and scanned the room. His eyes landed on Sadie. She did her best to try to read his expression, but his face gave no clue as to the status of her dear niece.

"Are you Lily's guardian?" he asked. Before Sadie could respond, Mark spoke on her behalf.

"We are her parents. This is her aunt. How is she?"

The doctor nodded and spoke with a straightforward candor that Sadie appreciated. "Lily was knocked unconscious and suffered a significant blow to the back of her head. According to the triage team, she began to regain her consciousness after approximately twenty minutes, which is a good sign. We have her sedated at the moment. Lily needed several stitches in her head and bandages on her leg and arm where she has road rash. They are currently doing an MRI to assess any potential brain trauma she may have endured. We will know more once we receive those results. While head trauma is not to be taken lightly, she is stable and, at this time, we have no reason to believe that she will not make a full recovery. Children often prove to be resilient."

"When can we see her?" Bridget asked.

The doctor scanned the clipboard in his hand before responding. "She should be finished with the scan in the next twenty minutes or so. After that she will be transferred to a room where you will be able to see her. Someone will be out to let you know where that is. Bear in mind that when she wakes, she will be quite groggy from the sedation. She may also be confused. Your presence in the room will be calming to her."

While Mark and Bridget settled into the worn chairs that lined the waiting room wall, Sadie opted to give them some time alone. Truthfully, she wasn't ready to face the sight of Lily. The doctor's assessment had been encouraging, but fear and guilt were clawing at her just below the surface. *What if the doctor was wrong and Lily doesn't survive? Or what if she suffers brain trauma from the injuries?* It was too much, too familiar. She had to get some space from the panic that was beginning to suffocate her.

She wandered the hospital halls aimlessly before stumbling upon the hospital chapel. The large cross above the double doors made that abundantly clear. In Sadie's heart, it felt like a physical battle of wills was taking place. One that told her to run in the opposite direction, and another that was nudging her to enter and find solace under that old wooden cross. The latter won out. Pushing open the heavy door, Sadie found the room to be empty. She slipped into the back row of chairs, buried her face in her hands, and allowed the emotions overtake her.

Surprisingly, anger was the emotion that bubbled to the surface. Anger at herself for not taking better care of her sweet niece. Anger that she was once again in a hospital where someone she loved was in critical condition. Anger that God would allow such suffering to happen to people he supposedly loved. She couldn't take it anymore. "How could you let this happen?" she shouted into the empty room as hot tears streamed from her eyes.

A voice behind her caused her to jump.

"If I had a dollar for every time I've heard someone shout that at these walls. The hospital seems to bring those frustrations out in people." The voice was connected to an older man, likely in his seventies. He was mostly bald, with patches of silver hair above his ears, and was using a cane to steady himself. The collar at his neck spoke to his occupation and the furrow in his brow spoke of his concern for her. He pulled a crumpled tissue from his pocket and offered it to Sadie.

"My apologies, I couldn't help but overhear. Mind if I join you?"

Embarrassed to have had a spectator to her emotional outburst, Sadie said nothing, but accepted the tissue and shifted down in the row as an invitation for the man to take a seat next to her.

"Now, since the likelihood of you getting an audible answer from God is rare," he cocked an eyebrow at her and added "not impossible mind you, but rare, how about you bend my ear a while as to what seems to be the problem. I've been told that I'm a good listener." The man rested both hands on his cane and leaned forward patiently waiting for a reply.

She released a slow breath and dabbed her eyes. Sadie was not typically the type to bare her soul to a stranger, but very little about the past month had been typical. What did she have to lose? Besides, he seemed harmless.

"My parents and I were in a car crash when I was nine. I was the only one who survived. They loved God, but He abandoned them. He abandoned me. Now here I am back in a hospital. A little girl's life might be hanging in the balance, and it's all my fault. It's not fair. Couldn't God, if He were loving and powerful, have prevented all this tragedy?" The anger that had initiated her outburst had dissolved. Desperation now dripped from her words. She felt completely helpless.

The man nodded his head knowingly and furrowed his brow. "You are completely right. He allowed your parents to be taken and for that child to be hurt. God has the power to end all the suffering on earth, and He doesn't. There have been many times in my life that I have wrestled with that very fact." He paused for a long time as though pondering his point. Sadie was shocked. His response was not what she expected, and she was beginning think that was all the spiritual insight he was going to offer when he tapped his cane on the floor and spoke again.

"But—and it's a big but—we don't believe in a God that makes our lives perfect or easy. In fact, quite the opposite. He allowed the worst possible thing to happen to his own Son who was the epitome of goodness. We believe that our life on this earth is just a vapour compared to the eternity that has been promised us, and in that place, there will be no pain or suffering."

Tilting his head upwards the man closed his eyes as though he were praying. "Isaiah 43:2 says, 'When you pass through the waters, I will be with you; and through the rivers they shall not overwhelm you; when you walk through fire you shall not be burned, and the flame shall not consume you'" (NRSV). He opened his eyes and looked at Sadie. "You hear that? He says *when*, not *if*. Pain in this life is a guarantee; our world is full of it. It's a consequence of our fallen nature, but we never have to face it alone. That is his promise."

"But how can I know that He will be with me or that there even is a better world after this one?" Sadie asked.

"That, my dear, is faith—the confidence in what we hope for and the assurance of that which we cannot see. The mystery of it all is that hope changes the one who hopes. It gives us the strength we need to endure this life and to believe that there is a purpose in all this."

His offering of hope felt like a lifeline. The world was a mess. She certainly could accept that. She had experienced it first-hand. The man did not try to explain or justify the suffering, he simply accepted it, but offered a hope that makes enduring worthwhile. It was a similar message to those she had heard before, but after all these years, Sadie finally felt ready to embrace it.

"I want that hope. I'm just so tired of feeling angry or overwhelmed by it all."

"Don't tell me. Tell Him."

"But what am I supposed to say?"

"Just be honest. God already knows what you're feeling, but He wants you to release your pain and anger to Him." With that, the old man stood up and was about to turn and leave, when he added, "And one more thing. I don't know you, but it sounds as though you need to forgive yourself. For the present and for the past. You are not to blame for these tragedies, and punishing yourself only hinders the good that you can offer the world."

At his words, Sadie could feel her stomach tense. She knew that he was right. For years she had carried the burden of sole survivor of that crash. Moments of joy or celebration were frequently clouded by the guilt she felt in living. And she certainly felt entirely to blame for what had happened to Lily. Sadie longed to be free of that guilt.

The man gingerly made his way out of the room, leaving Sadie alone once more.

As was beginning to become a habit whenever she thought of her parents, Sadie fingered the locket around her neck. She knew it was time. It was time to release it all—the anger, the guilt, the pain. It was time to trust that God was with her—He always had been.

Sadie closed her eyes and let a prayer settle on her heart: *God, I've been really angry at you for a long time. But I'm tired of carrying this anger with me. I'm sorry for the mess that I have made of everything and for not believing in your goodness. I see now that I need you. Lily needs you. Please heal her. Help me to trust that you will carry me through the waters that are threatening to drown me. Forgive me for turning my back on you. Teach me how to forgive myself and to let go of this guilt. Amen.*

As Sadie opened her eyes she realized that nothing about her situation had changed. Lily was still somewhere in the hospital. She was still an orphan. And yet, there was a fresh peace that settled on her. Her circumstances may be stormy, but God was with her, of that she now felt certain. That peace gave her the courage she needed to return to the Burgesses and face sweet Lily again.

Sadie stood in the doorway of Lily's hospital room. Bridget and Mark flanked the side of the large hospital bed and were holding Lily's hands. Noticing her, Mark stepped outside, gesturing that they should sit in the chairs along the wall. No one spoke for several minutes.

"How is she?" Sadie finally asked, breaking the silence.

"She's still sleeping, but the MRI report came back clear, praise the Lord. The doctor says that she has a concussion, but that they expect she should recover quickly. They will keep her overnight for monitoring and then will let her go home if all is clear. They expect that she will be pretty sore for a while, and we will have to watch her closely for any signs of residual trauma, but the doctor is hopeful that she will be back to herself before we know it."

"That is great news." Sadie stared at hospital walls as though they could give her the words to say. "Listen, Mark, I just want to say that I am so, so sorry. I should have been closer to her. I shouldn't have let her ride without a helmet."

Mark turned his body so that he was facing Sadie and spoke earnestly. "This is not your fault, Sadie. I said this earlier, but it is worth repeating. We don't blame you. It was an accident that could have happened to any one of us. Lily is in the hands of Jesus, and we trust Him completely with her, as scary as it is to see her hurt."

"I get it now. I'm sorry that it took something like this to wake me up, but I finally see that I can trust God when life gets rough. For so long, I was using my personal pain to push God away. I'm tired of running. I finally made the decision to surrender my life to Him." Sadie felt relieved to be able to now say those words aloud, solidifying her decision.

Before Sadie could say anything more, Mark enveloped her in a big bear hug. "That is incredible news. All of heaven is throwing a big party right now in your honour. How does it feel?"

Sadie pondered his question. "You know, in a lot of ways I feel the same. It doesn't change my circumstances, but there is peace that I am no longer trying to fight these battles in my own strength. And I have a deep hope now that there will be a day when we will be free of all this kind of suffering."

Mark leaned his elbows on his knees and rubbed his hands together. "You know, I can't imagine what it must have been like to be so young and facing such a traumatic event. You must have been so angry at God. I guess that part I can imagine. I loved my adopted family, but I went through a season where I felt a lot of anger toward Him, too. I didn't understand why He would allow me to be taken away from my birth parents. That anger ate me up inside."

Sadie nodded knowingly.

"But, God used people in my life to speak truth. I didn't want to listen at first. As you'd expect, my parents were the loudest voice, but for some reason kids find it much harder hear and accept their parents' wisdom. Surprisingly, it was my hockey coach who got through to me. My anger was starting to come out on the ice. I was hot-tempered and getting quick to drop the gloves during a game. He pulled me aside after a practice and told me that it was time to stop letting my anger control my life. He explained that anger was a response we use to distract us from a deeper pain, and he said it was time to face whatever was causing me pain and deal with it. I was a good kid, he said, but if I didn't figure out a way to manage my anger, he would bench me." Mark laughed.

"It was the tough love I needed to push me to see the truth about what was really angering me. I am grateful he didn't just write me off as a lost cause. It took a while to make peace with the reality of my situation, but it was a turning point."

The idea of anger being a pain response was new to Sadie. It certainly made sense. There was a lot of comfort in knowing that Mark understood and had walked a similar road. "You're right. I had been angry at God for a long time. It never made me want to fight someone though." Sadie laughed at the thought. "However, my anger definitely caused me to put up a lot of walls in my life."

"It won't get better overnight, but now you can let God carry those burdens for you. You don't have to face it alone."

She nodded as silence settled on them again. After a couple minutes Mark asked, "Would you like to see her?"

"Yes, please."

She sat opposite of Bridget and took Lily's hand in her own. Her tiny body looked so fragile in the large bed. Bandages were wrapped around her head and arm and wires ran from her chest to an assortment of monitors. The sight squeezed her heart, but it no longer made her despair and want to blame an apathetic God. Instead, she felt grateful. She was grateful that Lily's injuries were minor. She was grateful for the forgiveness of Bridget and Mark. But most of all, she was grateful that she now had hope that one day they could all experience a life without any sickness or pain.

Chapter Eighteen

"I'm sorry that we weren't able to take you on a tour of London," Mark said apologetically.

Sadie brushed off the apology with a wave of her hand. "Lily's health is far more important. I'm so glad she is mostly back to her old self. Besides, I have had more fun playing doctor with Lily over the past few days than I would have had in that stodgy, old city anyway," she said with a wink.

And she meant it.

No, she had not made it to London, but she felt no regrets about this journey. Her suitcase was filled with happy treasures from the adventures she had: a Prince William bobblehead; a handful of postcards of Oxford landmarks; a carefully packed hatbox containing a dainty, light blue feathered fascinator; a plastic dish with a dozen cookies from Ben's; and—perhaps the most precious of gifts—a stuffed bear dressed in Beefeater garb that had been a gift from Lily.

But more important than all those souvenirs was the change in her perspective. Traveler adventures were still of interest to her, but quiet, quality time with her family was far more valuable. *My family,* Sadie thought. *They truly are my family. What a difference only a few weeks can make.* The thought warmed her. She may not have her parents, but she was returning home to an aunt and uncle who loved her like their own and now she had a brother, sister-in-law, and niece whom she adored. In the past she may have looked at this as further reminders of all she had lost. Now, because of her relationship with Jesus, she knew that these people were gifts from God. They were proof that he had not abandoned her as she had once believed.

It took Sadie travelling to the other side of the ocean to realize all the things she just was not willing to see back home. For so long, she had closed herself off to being truly known or loved, as her anger toward God would force her to keep people at a distance. Now she finally felt ready to start fresh, to trust God with the pain of her past and with her future.

Sadie stuffed her now oversized bag into the boot of the car before she turned to exchange tearful goodbyes with her new family. The embraces carried with them promises of future visits and video calls. Lily was particularly concerned about Morris the Moose missing Sadie, to which point she made Sadie swear a solemn oath to check in on him weekly. Sadie promised, but only if Lily, in return, promised to never again ride a bike without a helmet, to which the young girl voraciously agreed.

As Mark pulled the car onto the street, Sadie looked back wistfully at the little house that had quickly become a home. Bridget and Lily were standing together at the door waving and blowing kisses. Sadie placed her hand to her lips and returned the gesture. With the kiss she sent a prayer of thankfulness heavenward for each one of them.

****

Her flight home proved to be uneventful. She was taking a red eye again, but at least this time, there would be no rush to recover from the return jet lag. There was also no doubt in her mind that Jack and Lynn would be so happy to have her home that they would be excited to lovingly dote on her—especially Lynn. *I bet she's been baking my favourites all day,* Sadie thought. They would also be delighted at the bag of goodies she had for them safely tucked in the bottom of her backpack.

There had been some extra time before her flight out of Heathrow Airport which she had capitalized on for some important, albeit last minute, souvenir shopping. Since Lily's recovery had taken precedence over their trip to London, there had been no opportunity to pick up anything special for her aunt and uncle. In spite of the limited options, Sadie was pleased with her purchases: a box of chocolates and a cheesy T-Shirt for Jack that read "Someone I love went to England and all I got was this lousy T-shirt," and a box of English breakfast tea and a cute, yellow wallet from Harrods for Lynn. Sadie had been so pleased to find that there was a Harrods in the airport. The luxury department store was so iconic that it had been on her list of things to see in London. The smaller storefront could not, of course, compare to the original which stretches over five acres, but that did not stop Sadie from taking a multitude of photos and splurging on a small, crossbody purse for herself.

As she turned her focus back to home, her mind wandered to Dawn. She wondered what her friend would think about the "come to Jesus" moment she had at the hospital chapel. Would Dawn scoff at her spirituality? Question her motives? No, that was not likely. Dawn was still Dawn and Sadie was still Sadie—best friends who had weathered a multitude of storms. Sadie was confident she would have the support of her friend. She chuckled to herself as she remembered the cryptic selfie that she had texted to Dawn at the airport. It was a picture of Sadie posed by a W|C sign in front of the washrooms. The caption read: "This might mean Water Closet to some, but for me this means 'World Changed.' Got so much to tell you, girl. See you soon!" It was just enough mystery for Dawn and the perfect homage to Sadie's first mix-up on British soil.

Sadie pulled her journal out of her carry-on bag squished in the space at her feet. Thumbing through its pages, she mentally relived the last three weeks, including many of its highs and lows that she had recorded in snippets of thoughts or funny stories or even, more recently, prayers. She paused on a page from one of her first days in Chipping Norton, tracing the words with her finger. "Go home with more than a double-decker bus keychain. Make memories that will last. Be a traveler, not a tourist." It was the advice that Bridget and Mark had given her at their trip to Elora's. Sadie was grateful that she had taken the advice to heart. She was returning home with a heart full of beautiful memories and a new perspective.

As Sadie continued flipping through the pages, her heart quickened. God was present in every memory—comforting her, protecting her, encouraging her. Not in a physical form, but through His people. Bridget's offering of kindness; Pia intercepting Oliver's advances; Mark's offering of forgiveness; the continued prayers for peace; even sweet Lily's outpouring of love. He had been with her all along. A silent tear slid down her cheek. *Thank you, God, for loving me, even when I had turned my back to you.* God was here. He had always been. She hugged her journal to her chest and, even though she was in an airplane surrounded by strangers, she let the holiness of the moment wash over her.

****

Sadie stood at the water's edge watching the moonlight dance across the glassy surface. All was still. Breathing in the salty air, Sadie drew strength from the peace she felt deep in her soul.

Oh Lord, thank you. Thank you for not giving up on me. Thank you for your goodness to me. Thank you for this place. Please give me the words to say and the courage to say them.

Dawn had not yet broken as Sadie walked to the dock. It was, in fact, closer to night than morning in her opinion, but the hour didn't matter since her internal clock was still on English time. She wouldn't be able to sleep anyway, not until she talked to Tom. The change that she felt in her heart had ushered peace into the corners of her world that had long been damaged and raw. She had spent the drive from the airport sharing all the details of her trip and her spiritual awakening with Lynn and Jack and they were, of course, thrilled that she had found such peace and assurance in God's goodness. But things with Tom were still unsettled. She needed to be honest with him. She needed him to know about what God had done in her life, not to win him back, but to restore that friendship.

Despite knowing she wouldn't be able to rest until she saw Tom, it took significant effort to keep her feet moving toward the docks. Not from exhaustion, but indecision. Would he think she was crazy? She certainly felt a little crazy at the moment. In the deepest part of her heart, Sadie knew that she had never completely closed the door on Tom. Just like Mark had explained, Sadie had masked her hurt feelings with anger. When the anger had dissipated, she was better able evaluate her pain. Tom had made a mistake in leading her on, but his intentions were good. She had been too blinded by her own anger at God to even hear him out. They were both to blame.

She wrapped her arms around her body to cut out the early morning chill and quickened her pace. There was no turning back now, but Sadie wondered if perhaps she should have spent more time evaluating her plan. She was less than fresh, and there was no guarantee that he would even be here, given that she still had no easy way to contact him. Tom had told her his workdays started at four in the morning. She had initially questioned the truthfulness of that claim, but now seeing the docks buzzing to life with fishermen preparing their boats for the day she had no doubts. Sadie only hoped that he hadn't yet left.

Her eyes scanned the boats moored at the dock, before landing on a familiar looking figure. There he was, handsome as ever even in his mucky fishing gear. He was hauling buoys onto the boat with great gusto. She called out to him, but he couldn't hear her over the sound of the motor. She tried again, louder this time. He perked up and looked around for the voice. When their eyes met, his expression was one of both confusion and joy.

He dropped what he was doing, deftly hopped from the boat to the dock and jogged over to her. It seemed as though he wanted to hug her, but he didn't. Instead, like a dog stopped by a shock collar, he stopped several feet from her as though hesitant to approach any further.

"You're back," he said, tentatively. "And you're here."

"I am. I literally just landed a few hours ago. I needed to see you."

"Me?"

Sadie inhaled slowly hoping to quell the butterflies in her stomach. She couldn't tell if it was what she was about to say or simply her proximity to Tom that had stirred those butterflies, but they were not making this any easier.

"Yes, you." She smiled at the way his hair stuck out from under his toque. "Tom, I need to apologize—"

"I'm the one who should be apologizing. I was judgmental and unfair to you. I knew that you still carried pain from your past, and I was pressuring you to be something you weren't ready for. It was not a good representation of Jesus or how He desires His followers to act. I should never have treated you the way that I did."

"Thank you for that. I forgive you." Tom's humble sincerity was endearing to Sadie. He was not trying to make excuses for himself but owned up to his failings. There weren't many guys she knew who would have the maturity or self-awareness to do the same. Now it was her turn to be vulnerable.

"I wasn't willing to listen to you before, Tom, and for that I am sorry. It was easier to just shut you out. For so long, the pain of my parents' passing and my anger at God dictated how I lived my life. I pushed people away because it was easier than having their sympathy remind me of all I had lost. Some things happened on my trip that forced me to face the fact that my pain doesn't deny the existence of a good God. Rather, His willingness to redeem the mess despite our constant failures is proof of how good He is."

Tom was looking at her intently now, hanging on her every word. Sadie continued, "Everything you told me finally makes sense. I decided to trade my anger for peace and my pain for hope. I decided to follow Jesus."

Tom said nothing, but the wide smile on his face spoke volumes as he enthusiastically pulled her into an embrace. After a moment, he pulled away but held her at arm's length, his hands on her shoulders staring into her eyes. Sadie wondered if he might kiss her, but instead he tilted his head upwards toward the starry sky and prayed. "Father, thank you for bringing your child back home to you. Restore her peace and give her hope for the future, whatever that may bring."

In the past Sadie might have been uncomfortable with his spontaneous benediction, but she was becoming more accustomed to Tom's spiritual openness. It felt like a fitting way to usher in this fresh start to their friendship.

"I am so happy for you. Thank you for coming down here in the middle of the night to share that with me," Tom said, then with an impish grin he added, "I thought you might be here for a lobster fishing lesson."

Sadie chuckled. She appreciated his sense of humour. It always set her at ease. In a bold move, Sadie slid her small hand into his and gave it a squeeze. For several minutes they stood hand in hand, the stars their audience and the dock bustling to life their background music. There were no plans made or declarations spoken, but the salty air carried with it the promise of hope for their future.

Too soon, Tom returned to his boat for a day on the ocean. He waved to her as he and his uncle sailed off. There would be lots more time to talk and process all that had happened. For now, Sadie was in much need of a shower and some decent sleep, which may or may not happen depending on how long before Dawn came over for a full explanation of the "W|C" picture. Aunt Lynn and Uncle Jack would be anxiously waiting to see her pictures and hear all her stories. The day promised to be full.

Instead of returning to her car right away, Sadie sat on the edge of the dock and watched as the sun slowly forced the darkness to flee, something she had never done. Behind her, shops were beginning to open their doors. A jogger ran past, his rhythmic steps causing the dock to rumble. In the distance, she could hear a rousing sea shanty being played from one of the boats. For the first time, being here at the ocean's edge, life felt full of hope.

"It's a new day," Sadie whispered as she gazed across the vista at the golden orb inching its way up the horizon.

She felt it in her soul. Finally at peace with all the chapters that came before, a fresh chapter of her story was beginning, and she could not wait to see where it would take her.

Acknowledgments

It is hard to believe that this project is finally complete. Writing a novel in the middle of a pandemic with three young children at home has proven to be a challenge, and one I could not have accomplished without much help and support.

Thank you to my fantastic editor, Loral Pepoon. Not only have you lovingly worked with me to perfect this book, but you have also patiently answered all my questions about the editing and publishing process.

Thank you to my cover designer, Lisa Thompson, for bringing my vision for the cover to life.

To my writing inspiration, Robin Jones Gunn—your stories have been foundational to my life and have inspired me on this writing journey. Thank you for the way that you lavish love on your readers and point them to Jesus.

To my beta readers, Vanessa Chupp, Sarah Piercy, and Karlie Bennett—thank you for all your feedback and encouragement.

To all my friends in Orillia and Moncton—through many different seasons your friendships have been life-giving to me.

A big thanks all my family and friends who support and encourage me in my writing. You have been my biggest cheerleaders. Thank you to my siblings, Jerrica and Taylor. You have both taught me so much about the art of storytelling; Jerrica—in telling stories that captivate an audience and make people laugh, and Taylor—in using the written word to paint a picture and take the reader on an emotional journey. Mom and Dad, thank you for always encouraging me to follow my dreams. I love you dearly. To Jeremy, my husband and best friend, your belief in me has never wavered. Thank you for making space for me to pursue writing and for all your wisdom throughout the process.

And to my Heavenly Father, thank you for the gift of words. May I always use them to honour You.